"MISTER, EITHER YOU GOT A HANKERING TO DIE OR ELSE YOU'RE PLUMB LOCO."

Cameron stepped away from the bar. "I ain't looking for opinions, I'm looking to hire some men to help fix up my place."

"Hell, there ain't nothing left of that two-bit outfit but dust and ashes," another cowhand called out.

Cameron stared at the second man. "Sounds like you're working for Muleshoe. If I catch any Muleshoe man on my range, I aim to shoot first and talk later."

More cowhands stepped away from the bar—more Muleshoe men. The first man said, "You're a damned fool, Cameron. You should've never come back."

"Here's where I belong," Cameron said flatly, "and it's here I'll stay."

The Muleshoe men advanced on him; the first cowhand smiled. "And it's here you'll get buried. . . ."

SIGNET Westerns by Ray Hogan

The Renegade Gun

RAY HOGAN

Ⓢ

A SIGNET BOOK

NEW AMERICAN LIBRARY

TIMES MIRROR

PUBLISHER'S NOTE

This novel is a work of fiction. Names, characters, places, and incidents either are the product of the author's imagination or are used fictitiously, and any resemblance to actual persons, living or dead, events, or locales is entirely coincidental.

CHAPTER 1

~~~~~~~~~~~~~~~~~~~~~~~~~~~~~~~~~~~~

When the westbound stagecoach skidded to a halt in front of Wolf Springs' Emporia Hotel late that hot summer morning, the off door flung open immediately, and a tall, hard-bitten, sun-scorched man stepped out into the spinning dust.

He had no baggage, and hesitating until the choking pall had cleared somewhat, he brushed the sweat-stained hat he was wearing to the back of his head, and let his glance run the weathered facades of the false-fronted buildings lining the canyon-like street. As he did his pale eyes crinkled at the corners; habitually narrowed from countless days in glaring sunlight, they seemed to become more hard-surfaced, and the grim, straight line of his mouth grew tighter. A lethal-looking man, he gave the impression not only of invulnerability and great strength, but of violence, deep-seated and suppressed.

"John Cameron?"

At the brusque question the traveler pivoted slowly to face the porch of the hotel. The slim, elderly man looking

5

down at him was wearing the star of town marshal. He had evidently been waiting inside the hostelry, and had emerged upon the arrival of the stage.

"That's me," Cameron replied, coolly sizing up the lawman.

Somewhere in his late fifties, or possibly early sixties, with long, shoulder-length white hair, curving mustache, and pointed beard, he had small black eyes that were sharp as bayonet yucca. This was the new lawman Cameron had heard about; the marshal who had been in charge, and for whom Cameron had occasionally served as deputy, had died while he was away.

"Name's Stanwyck—Nathan Stanwyck. I'm the law here—and I'm warning you right now that I won't stand for no trouble."

Cameron brushed at the beads of sweat gathered on his forehead. "Sid Mason send you to tell me that?" he asked in a voice colored with sarcasm.

Stanwyck stiffened angrily. "I don't take orders from him or nobody else, mister!" he snapped. "I'm my own man."

John Cameron shrugged. "Pleasures me to hear that, but I reckon I'll wait a spell before I make up my mind that it's true . . . You got anything else to say?"

"I have. I know you're back here looking for vengeance—aiming to square your hate for Mason, but—"

"Vengeance's got nothing to do with it. And I reckon the same goes for hate. I've got a right to hate Sid Mason for framing me into the pen, but I kind of got it out of my system during the three years I was there."

Stanwyck's smile was humorless. "Maybe you'll find somebody that'll believe that, Cameron—I sure as hell won't! And while we're talking about the pen you might as well know that I was against your getting turned loose. You were sent up there to serve ten years for killing that boy, and—"

"That boy as you call him was twenty-five years old, and his name was Brand Redmon."

"Whatever. Point is he was unarmed, and you shot him down in cold blood—no matter that you were serving as a deputy at the time."

"He had a gun. He drew on me when I went to arrest him. Somebody took it, made it look like he was unarmed."

"I know the story, and what you claimed. The jury and the judge didn't see it that way."

"Sure—a jury scared to buck Sid Mason, and a judge bought and paid for by him. How do you figure I could get a pardon from a ten-year sentence when I'd served only three years if the governor and the warden hadn't decided the whole thing was crooked?"

Stanwyck considered that briefly, and then shook his head indifferently. "That don't interest me none, Cameron. What does is your coming back here to my town all cocked and primed to stir up a lot of hell. Can see that's what you've got in mind just by looking at you. Now, I ain't going to put up with it. I'm asking you straight out, to climb back into that stage and keep going, let things be around here. I know I can't order you to, but it'd be best for everybody—"

"Even me?" Cameron asked dryly.

"Specially you. There's nothing here for you now, so why—"

"Everything I've got's here. My ranch and—"

"Your place is just ruins. Burned down one night. Was drifters set fire to it, folks figure."

Cameron laughed, a harsh, derisive sound in the hot,

still air. Although there was no one else in sight along the street the hush was proof that all activity in Wolf Springs had suspended, and every person within visual range was watching.

"You're a damn fool if you swallow that!" he said. "Sid Mason had some of his bunch put a torch to it."

"You can't back up a statement like that," the lawman countered.

"No, I don't expect you ever will come up with proof of any of the things Mason and his Muleshoe outfit have done to this valley—not the killings, or the times they burned out some homesteader or rancher so's he could get his hands on their land; or the stunts they pulled like poisoning a water hole, or setting fire to grass, shooting cattle and horses—"

Stanwyck raised a hand. "Never mind! Talk comes mighty cheap. Anytime a man brings me something solid to go on, I'll do my duty."

"Proof's something you'll never get, Marshal! Mason's got this country by the short hair. Everybody living in Red Rock Valley is scared to buck him, and won't open their mouths no matter what they see happening."

"And you're aiming to change that?"

"I figure to be one who'll stand up to Mason and his bunch of hired guns—and if things work out right, break him, and drive him clear out of the valley before I'm done."

"Best you change that to 'before you're dead' because that's likely how you'll wind up."

Cameron smiled wryly. "Seems I just heard you say that Sid and his outfit didn't ever break any laws. Now, killing me—"

"Damn it—that's not what I said!" Stanwyck declared

impatiently. "Told you there never was any proof of them doing it—but I'm done talking to you," the lawman said, again swiping at the sweat on his angry features. He glanced down the street where now half a dozen men were to be seen gathered in the shade of a small tree—a better vantage point from which to watch, apparently.

"Want you to keep this in mind," Stanwyck continued. "You stir up a lot of trouble for me around here and I'll see what I can do about getting that pardon of yours revoked, and sending you back up to the pen. I expect it can be done."

Cameron drew himself up slowly and folded his arms across his chest. Clad in a worn, colorless shirt, faded cord pants, scarred, run-down boots, and battered hat, his appearance was in sharp contrast to that of the well-dressed lawman.

"Maybe you'll try, Stanwyck," he said in a low, threatening voice, "but not you or anybody else will ever put me inside those walls again. Best you remember that."

"You're the one who'd better keep a few things in mind—one of them being that you ain't got a friend left in this part of the country, and if you start out after Sid Mason with that damn fool idea of busting him, and running him out of the valley, you'll learn mighty quick that you'll be on your own. What's more, you make one move that I figure's against the law, you'll answer to me.

"Now I'll say it again—best thing you can do is keep on going, but I can see you're too wooden-headed to take that advice, so I'll warn you once more; leave things be. Don't stir up trouble—and you'll be smart to keep right on leaving off your gun like you are."

"Reckon I'll have to disappoint you again, Marshal. Aim to change that right away."

The lawman shrugged, sighed. "Expected you would, and it'd still be a good idea if you'd forget it. But I've had my say," he finished, and pivoting abruptly on a heel, re-entered the hotel.

Cameron's attention remained on the dust-clogged screen door behind which Nathan Stanwyck had disappeared. The lawman was right in one thing; he'd find no friends in Wolf Springs—none except Ketty Griffin. As his thoughts shifted to her some of the grim, hard lines in his weathered face softened.

Ketty had been a part of his life, and had remained so even after he had met and become smitten by Darcy Bellamy, who had come to live with her father and work in the family restaurant. Subsequently she had agreed to Cameron's proposal of marriage, but that had changed abruptly when he had let himself fall into Sid Mason's trap, and was soon after sent off to prison.

Darcy had turned from him then, but Ketty had never changed. Later, in the dark stillness of the bitter nights behind the walls of the penitentiary, Cameron had cursed himself for the fool he'd been. With Darcy—beautiful beyond words—it had been sheer bewitchment—infatuation he thought the word was. Where the equally lovely Ketty was concerned, he realized then that she was the woman he wanted to be with the rest of his life.

Ketty had never forsaken him, had been his only contact with home and the valley he loved so. She had written to him numerous times, doing her best to brighten up his days with letters. Darcy had written to him once during the three years that he was struggling to survive in a hellhole of brutality, searing heat, numbing cold, and unending days of breaking rock, and that not a missive of encouragement, but one advising him that she was marrying Sid Mason.

That most of all drove home to John Cameron the truth of his relationship with the two women. Darcy had been but a passing fancy, a mirage of beauty that captivated him but was actually without substance. Ketty Griffin, on the other hand, was there all the time, warm and sure and waiting.

Coming about, John Cameron brought his flat gaze back to the street. Behind him he heard the stagecoach driver come out of the hotel, climb up onto the seat of the vehicle, and prepare to continue his westward journey, but the sounds registered only vaguely on Cameron's mind. He was resuming his review of the dusty lane, and of the structures that lined it, which had been interrupted by Marshal Nathan Stanwyck.

He could see little change. Major's Hardware, the General Store of George Morgan; Harry Walton's name still graced the Gun Shop; the Cattleman's Bank, Kurtzman's Bakery, Sweeney's Livery Stable, Taylor's Blacksmith Shop, the High Ridge Saloon & Restaurant where Ketty worked; Isaiah Treadwell's Boot & Shoe Shop, the meat market, Sol's Clothing Store, the Cottonwood Saloon—the Rainbow Restaurant.

There was change after all. Once the Rainbow had been known as Bellamy's Restaurant—run by Tom Bellamy, and taken over upon his death by Darcy. That was when he had met her, Cameron recalled, and where she still was when he had gone off to serve his time for a killing that was not, as they had claimed, a murder.

Later Ketty wrote that Darcy had sold the restaurant, probably at Sid Mason's insistence. A man as proud and powerful as he was—a man who boasted openly that before he was finished he intended to own a million acres of land upon which he would run two hundred thousand head of cattle—could not permit his wife to work even in her own business.

Wolf Springs had come to a halt, had stagnated just as Cameron had maintained it would. There were no new merchants, no new homes among those clustered around the small Methodist church—still in need of paint—at the edge of town, and no new ranches or homesteads in the valley. That had been the case even before he had gone away, and that fact, according to one of Ketty's letters, had not changed. It was as if a wall had been erected around the area, one efficiently maintained by Sid Mason's Muleshoe riders for the sole purpose of excluding any and all newcomers while within Mason was ruthlessly acquiring the land of those already there by any means necessary.

Would Cameron have any greater success in convincing the few ranchers and homesteaders who were still holding out than he'd had before falling victim to Sid Mason's power? No one could supply the answer to that, Cameron knew; only by getting in touch with them, along with those who had already been dispossessed by Mason, and rallying them to stand with him against the owner of giant Muleshoe, would he find out.

And that determination, solidifying itself within him during his time behind the walls of prison, was his reason for being, his reason for returning to Wolf Springs and the Red Rock Valley—and resuming the fight against Sid Mason. He would, in whatever way necessary, break the man, drive him out of the valley, and thereby put an end to his unremitting, relentless devouring of the land.

Such had become an obsession with John Cameron, a

crusade to rid the valley—his homeland—of the blight that, like the lovely flowered but deadly bindweed, was strangling it; he would do it—with or without help.

Settling his hat forward on his head, allowing the irregular brim to better shade his eyes, Cameron started down the dusty, heat-trapped street for the High Ridge— and Ketty. It would be good to see her again—fully aware now of how much she meant to him—take her in his arms, talk to her, revel in the sound of her voice again. It was something he had looked forward to for months, and for the time being all else would have to wait.

Glancing to right and left Cameron took note of the faces peering at him from behind glassed windows and open doorways, but he accorded them no sign of recognition, simply continuing on his way. And then abruptly his step slowed. The hard glint of metal in the sunlight, coming from a passageway lying between two of the buildings, had caught his attention, and sent a warning racing through him.

He reacted instinctively and instantaneously, throwing himself to one side, and going to hands and knees just as a gunshot shattered the silence that blanketed the town.

Cursing, Cameron lunged to his feet, and rushed toward the building immediately to his left—the hardware store of Pete Major's. He had no weapon, none of any kind, but that fact did not deter him or diminish the soaring anger that was pouring through him. He wanted only to reach the passageway, seize the would-be bushwhacker, and tear him apart.

He was conscious of people coming into the street as he rushed toward the mouth of the opening, of shouts, and the thud of boot heels behind him in the direction of the hotel. The thought: *that will be the marshal*, flashed through his mind and out again, making no impression.

Cameron drew near the passageway, slowed his head-long charge. Caution, at last, was overtaking him. Dropping into a crouch he paused at the corner of the near building, and then still low, literally threw himself into the passageway.

Another curse ripped from his lips. There was no one there. Not halting, Cameron ran the length of the weed-littered corridor to is opposite end, and again using care, paused and eased himself forward to where he could see into the intersecting alleyway. There was no sign of the bushwhacker. After taking his shot, he had quickly disappeared.

Still glowing with anger, Cameron turned, retracing his steps to the street. Nathan Stanwyck, his face dark and stern, awaited him.

"I reckon you can see what I meant when I said you was trouble!" he said. "You're in town ten minutes and the shooting starts."

"Go talk to Sid Mason about it," Cameron replied coldly, letting his eyes touch the knot of bystanders grouped off to one side. Sweeney, the livery stable owner, was among them, along with Pete Major, Harry Walton, and Aaron Wilson, the banker. None spoke; they all simply stared at him.

"How could you know it was Mason?" Stanwyck said, shaking his head. "Did you see him?"

"It was Mason's doing—you can figure on it," Cameron declared in the same restrained voice. "Sent one of his hired hands to pick me off, put me in the boneyard before I could cause him trouble."

The lawman spat. "Hell, you're only guessing, Cameron—and I ain't sure you're all that important to Sid Mason in the first place."

"Maybe so—"

"I expect from here on out anything that happens to you, you'll blame it on the Muleshoe outfit—from getting throwed by a horse to getting stung by a bee. It could've been somebody else besides one of Mason's boys that took a shot at you. Like I told you—you've got no friends around here now—and when a man's short on friends, he's usually long on enemies."

Cameron swept the marshal with a disdainful look. "Could be," he murmured, and stepping back into the street, continued on his way to the High Ridge.

CHAPTER 2

~~~~~~

Cameron saw Ketty a few moments later. She was standing on the narrow porch that fronted the High Ridge along with several others who had apparently been drawn into the open by the gunshot.

She was slightly forward of the rest, almost on the edge of the landing, and his first full look at her lifted his spirits and set his pulse to racing. Ketty was wearing a bright yellow dress cut not too low at the neck, but just enough to expose the arches of her full breasts, and of a length that covered her ankles. A circlet of gold was about her throat, and a matching bracelet was on her wrist.

Her hair, a deep chestnut that glinted in the sunlight, was gathered about her head, and softly framed her face. Even from the distance Cameron thought he could see the blueness of her eyes, but there was no question as to the smoothness of her features, the full lips, and the creaminess of her skin. She was just as he had envisioned her a thousand or more times in those past years.

Ketty did not always look that way, he knew. She had fixed herself up special for his return. That pleased him, and heightened his desire and need for her. How could he have ignored her for Darcy Bellamy—or any other woman? She was exactly what he had always hoped for and dreamed of. Together they could—

John Cameron's thoughts came to a stop, sobering his lean features, dimming the light that had brightened his heart and soul. There was no future for Ketty and him, at least not until he had acomplished what he had sworn to do. When that was done—and he still lived—then he could go to Ketty and ask her to share his life. To do so now, with nothing but dire probabilities facing him, would be cruel.

Oblivious to the men on the High Ridge's porch, and of several other persons now in the street, Ketty stepped down into the dust, and hurried to meet him. He took her into his arms, kissed her, held her close, and then released her when she spoke.

"Let's go to my place. This is not the—"

He nodded as she let her words fade, and ignoring the stares of onlookers, placed an arm around her slender waist, and went with her to the small, two-room house at the edge of town.

Entering, Ketty closed the door despite the trapped heat, and again went into his arms.

"Oh, John—I'm so glad you're back—that you're home!"

"No happier about it than I am," he replied tightly. "Been looking forward to this ever since the first day I spent inside the walls. Hellhole like that makes a man think of all the time he's wasted—the things he's missed. Ketty, I—"

She drew back expectantly. "Yes?"

"—want to say this. I was a damn fool for not asking you to be my wife years ago. It was one of my big mistakes."

"Don't think about it now—it's all over and done with." Ketty waited out a long minute, and when he said no more, continued: "Expect you're hungry. I've some frying meat, and the fixings."

Cameron nodded, and reluctantly releasing the woman, let his arms fall from about her to his sides.

"My gun?" he said, that subject coming to his mind in the next moment. "You said in a letter that Darcy had given it to you."

Wordless, Ketty crossed to a closet in the rear of the combination sitting and bedroom. Pushing aside the curtain that covered its opening, she obtained his belted pistol.

"Your money's in the holster.

He took the weapon from her, one of the newer-model Colt forty-fives, which he'd purchased from the gun company's drummer not long before he was sent away. Fondling the pistol for several moments, he flipped open the loading gate, spun the empty cylinder, and then began to load the chambers with cartridges from the belt.

"I'd've felt a hell of a lot better out there in the street a bit ago if I had been wearing this," he said in a regretful tone.

Ketty, busy adding wood to the firebox of the stove, and placing a larded spider over one of the open holes, paused, and faced him.

"Who was it that shot at you, John? Did you get a look at him? I was so afraid—and then when I saw the marshal talking to you—"

"Whoever it was run before I could get to where he was

hiding. Can bet on it being one of Sid Mason's hired hands."

The pistol loaded, Cameron started to thrust it into the holster, and remembering what the girl had said, reached into the leather sheath with two fingers and withdrew the roll of currency he'd placed there. He didn't bother to count it—a bit less than two hundred dollars, he recalled. Tucking the money into a pocket in his shirt, he slid the forty-five into the oiled holster and laid the gear on a small table nearby. Turning then, Cameron settled into one of the two calico-padded rocking chairs and glanced around.

The rooms were much as he remembered them; worn, flowered carpet on the living and bedroom floor, bare but well-scrubbed planks of the kitchen area where there were also facilities for dining. The same familiar prints hung on the walls, and the curtains over the windows, clean and frilly, were as before; the same quilted bedspread made of squares from many different materials, the half-dozen books on a shelf, one of which he recalled was the Bible of Ketty's dead mother.

The kitchen stove, which doubled as a source of heat on cold days as well as for preparing meals, was clean and had been recently blacked. Cans and boxes of food, arranged in orderly manner, lined the shelves of one wall, and he noted that the hand pump that he had personally installed for Ketty's convenience shortly after they had become acquainted some five years ago appeared to be in good working condition. She paused before it to lever a quantity of water into the coffeepot.

"What do you plan to do?" Ketty's voice was low, tense, almost as if she feared to hear the answer to the question. "You wrote only a few times, and you never once said what you intended to do when you got back."

"Nothing's changed," Cameron said flatly. "Feel the same as always about Sid Mason. I'm going to drive him out of the country."

Ketty dumped a handful of crushed coffee beans into the pot and set it on the stove. The meat in the frying pan was now beginning to sizzle, and the smell of it in the confines of the small house was pleasant and tantalizing.

"You say that like it was nothing, John—no more of a chore than ricking wood or feeding the livestock."

"That's about all it amounts to, far as I'm concerned—"

Ketty turned back to the stove, and removing the lid from the frying pan began to slice into it the potatoes she had previously boiled to tenderness. Outside in the yard a mocking-bird was filling the day with his trills and arias.

"I—I don't want you to think I'm against what you aim to do—but I'm not sure you realize how things are here in the valley now."

Cameron rose, walked to the door, opened it, and allowed some of the heat building from the stove's activity to escape.

"I doubt if there's much change," he said. "Mason's still hogging everything, stomping on anybody that gets in his way. That's the same as it always was."

"Yes, I know, but there are only a few ranchers and farmers left that he hasn't taken over. I don't think any of them will have the courage to stand by you."

"What do they figure to do? Just set there like a cottontail letting a coyote chew it up?"

Ketty shrugged. "They probably figure to just hang on, hope Mason won't want their land."

"Fooling themselves," Cameron said, staring out into the hot, late morning. The mockingbird had hushed, and now the only sound to break the quiet was insects clicking in the weeds nearby, and sparrows chattering busily in the dust of the chicken yard.

"You can't blame them," Ketty said, beginning to set the table. "Those men—hard cases all of them—that Sid has working for him won't stop at—"

"Who are they?" Cameron broke in. "It the same bunch?"

"Bear Kugan's one. He's still sort of the leader. And there's the Leavitt brothers—Dan and Curly. And Quint Redmon—"

"Brand's brother?"

"Yes. The only new one I can think of is a man named Ben Lancaster. Heard it said that he is an outlaw, and wanted for killing somebody, somewhere. They say he's a real bad one—like Kugan."

"Seems Mason's keeping himself pretty well fixed with gunmen. Aims to get that million-acre ranch he's after, I reckon, come fire or flood."

"Sid's just the same as always," Ketty agreed. "I won't say that I think you ought to forget this—this feud you have with him—because I know it's something you feel you have to do, but I worry that—"

She broke off, paused, watched him turn away from the door, cross to the kitchen, and sit down to the table.

"I have to do it, Ketty. It's like there was something chawing at my insides, and won't let up until I've done what I figure needs doing. It's not vengeance like most folks'll probably think it is. I don't have much to gain for myself by breaking Sid Mason and driving him out—or killing him. It's only that, for the good of the country, it has to be done."

Ketty was studying his tense features, worry in her eyes. "You talk of killing Sid—what if he or one of his hired guns kills you?"

John Cameron shrugged. "Could happen, of course, but they'd not find the job easy. I learned to survive while I was in the pen—expect I can outside. Anyway, I have to go ahead with what I've sworn to do."

"Sworn—to who?"

"To myself, Ketty."

The woman was silent for a long minute, and then sighing, said: "No matter how careful you are, how expert you've become at staying alive, you still could get killed. You can't be on guard every minute of the day and night. Besides, you don't owe folks around here anything! They wouldn't stand up and fight with you before—they're not likely to now. Can't you see that, John?"

Ketty's voice had risen slightly, was almost to a desperation pitch. Cameron seemed not to notice.

"That's something I'll have to find out," he said. "Who's left?"

Again the woman sighed. "Oh, half a dozen homesteaders—most of them west of here. And then there's Tom Lear and Claude Ivey—they're still hanging on to their ranches. I guess the biggest one of them that Sid Mason hasn't taken over yet is Lige Davidson."

"That's enough to start. Can stir them up, make them see what's ahead for them if they don't fight."

"They wouldn't before," Ketty pointed out for the second time. "I can't see them changing now."

"Maybe they will. They've had a chance to see what happened to their neighbors—and that I was right when I tried to get them together four years ago. Could be they've grown a little backbone."

Ketty smiled wryly. "I hope so."

He grinned also, a hard, rueful grimace. "Expect I'll find out fast enough. Sure be obliged to you, Ketty, if you'll pass the word that I want to see them—and anybody else that's got a stake in the valley—at my ranch tomorrow—by noon if possible. Want to lay out my plans, tell them what I aim to do."

"What will—what can you do?" Ketty interrupted, frowning. "I can't see how you—"

"I need to find out who Mason's pushing to sell out, or that he's about to crack down on. If I can get that information then I'll try to bring everybody I can together and we'll be waiting for the Muleshoe bunch, and make a stand."

Ketty moved the frying pan to one side of the stove, and taking up the coffeepot, filled the two cups she had placed on the table with steaming black liquid. That done, she took the already baked bread that had been warming in the oven, along with a dried apple pie, and set them before Cameron. After that she filled his plate with meat and potatoes from the spider.

"I used to think about the meals you'd put on the table," Cameron said, taking a swallow of the coffee. "Was like remembering Christmas. The stuff they fed us up there in the pen was swill."

Ketty nodded, began to eat, daintily picking at her food. "I missed your not coming here, John—more than you'll ever know—even before you went away."

She was thinking of Darcy Bellamy. He had taken only a few meals at Bellamy's Restaurant until Darcy came. After that he could be found there often, had, in fact, become not only a regular patron, but a successful suitor for Darcy's hand as well.

"That was one of the mistakes I made," Cameron said, leaning toward the girl and looking at her closely. "I was a fool."

"What about her? What about Darcy?"

The words came out in a rush. He shook his head. "She means nothing to me—married or not. Not now, and I don't figure she really did three years ago. I reckon I was sort of blinded by it all—by her. After I left I realized it was only you that counted. Is she happy being the wife of Sid Mason?"

Ketty, still toying with her food, stirred slightly. "I suppose. I see her now and then on the street or in one of the stores. We don't talk much. After all she's the wife of the biggest rancher in this part of the country, and I work in a saloon."

"She's not a better woman for that, I know. You work in the restaurant part of a saloon, not around the bar, and unless you've changed while I was away, you're straight as an Apache arrow."

"I've not changed," Ketty replied. "Where will you spend the night? I doubt if your place is livable."

"Probably right, but I aim to ride out, have a look. Could be I can fix it up a bit."

"You're welcome to stay here, John, just like you did before, well, before things came between us . . . We had good times in those days."

"We will again, you can bet on it. Just let me get this thing with Mason settled, then we can start all over again." Cameron hesitated, added: "Figure to ask you something when that time comes."

"Why not now?"

"Can't—wouldn't be right. For now just trust me, and have faith in me—and keep on being my friend. Expect you're the only one I have."

"There might be others, only they're afraid to be friendly with you. Do you have to leave right away—go out to your ranch, I mean?"

"No, I'd like to stay around, spend some time with you after we're through eating. Lot of things I'd like to talk about, and make up for. Are they looking for you back at the High Ridge soon?"

"Told Kingman I'd be taking most of the day off. He expects me by suppertime, though."

"Good—that'll give us a while. Maybe the day will come soon when you won't have to hold a job."

Ketty, cup of coffee halfway to her lips, hesitated, involuntarily glancing at the holstered pistol lying on the library table in the adjoining room. A faint shudder passed through her.

"I hope so," she murmured, but there was a strain of doubt in her voice.

CHAPTER 3

〰〰〰〰〰〰〰〰〰〰〰〰〰〰〰〰〰〰〰〰

Around four o'clock in the afternoon Cameron left Ketty Griffin's small house, and returning to Wolf Springs' main street, bent his steps toward Morgan's General Store.

The time spent with Ketty had brightened his hopes and filled him with pleasure, and although the remembrance of the attempt on his life only a few hours earlier kept him at a continual alert, there was almost a light-heartedness to him as he strode purposefully along in the withering heat. He was conscious, too—and again—of the covert attention his passing was being accorded, and it both amused and irritated him. They were looking upon him as their enemy, he knew, when in reality his sole intention was to help them, to save them from the oblivion that a town, owned and controlled by Sid Mason, would bring. They would realize that when it was all over.

Reaching the store, Cameron climbed the half-dozen plank steps to the landing, all but covered with displays of washtubs, water buckets, secondhand furniture, yard tools, and such, and made his way through the melange to the screen door. Pulling it back, he stepped inside.

Morgan was standing behind the counter that extended across the rear of the large, well-stocked room. It was apparent he had seen Cameron approaching. John, halting just within to allow his eyes to adjust, and to enjoy momentarily the good smells of the store's merchandise, continued then toward the back of the store.

Reaching the counter, Cameron eyed Morgan waiting coolly with arms folded across his chest. Once George Morgan had been his closest friend—both being bachelors— but as was the case with everyone else in the settlement that he knew, excepting Ketty Griffin, a wall had sprung up between them when Sid Mason let it be known that anyone opposing his determination to build a million-acre cattle ranch was an enemy, and should be so considered by all; left unsaid was the not so subtle implication that anyone who did not agree and comply would suffer the consequences.

It was clear to Cameron that Morgan's position had not changed, but he said: "Howdy, George. It's good to see you again."

Morgan merely nodded, murmured, "John," and let his greeting end there.

At that Cameron's shoulders stirred indifferently, and he glanced about. The cost of friendship was dear, he thought—too much for George Morgan to pay.

"Aim to fix up my place a bit," he said. "Not much at first—just enough so's I can live on it. I'll be needing supplies. My credit good here?"

Morgan brushed at his jaw, and frowned. A tall, thin man with small dark eyes and outsized mustache, he wore the customary denim bib apron over his everyday clothes.

"Not so sure that's a good idea," he said finally, in a slow, hesitant way. "Was told there's hardly anything left of your place."

"Bunkhouse is probably still standing, being made mostly of sod, and with a dirt roof. The fire them drifters set wouldn't've hurt it much."

There was a touch of sarcasm in Cameron's words. Morgan took note of it but chose to ignore it. "Probably so. If you're planning to—"

The storekeeper checked himself, shifted his attention to the front entrance. Cameron turned. A hard smile drew down the corners of his mouth when he recognized the two men entering—Peter Major of the hardware store, and Aaron Wilson, the town banker.

The pair hurried in, took up a position at the counter, neither man speaking. Watching them through shuttered eyes, Cameron felt the last of his lightheartedness dwindle and slip away.

"What brings you back here, Cameron?" Wilson demanded in his calm but insistent voice. "You're not welcome in Wolf Springs—you damn well know that!"

"That Sid Mason talking?" Cameron asked dryly.

The banker's mouth tightened beneath his thick mustache. A squat, thick man in a baggy blue suit, white collarless tie closed at the neck with a copper button, he wore round, steel-rimmed spectacles that made his eyes look small.

"That's me, and the folks of this town talking," Wilson replied, and turned to Morgan. "What's he want, George?"

The storekeeper said, "Supplies. Aiming to fix up his place, and live there, he says."

"Best you forget that," Pete Major said after the several moments of silence following Morgan's words had passed. "If you're smart you'll keep on moving. There's nothing here in the valley for you."

Cameron smiled bleakly. "Expected you to look at it that way. Fact is everything is here. My ranch—"

"Ranch!" the hardware store man echoed. "Hell, there ain't nothing left of it but ashes! What you're really doing back here is to get even with Sid Mason—maybe kill him."

"No," Cameron said quietly, "not to get even, but to drive him out of the country."

"There—you have it!" Wilson shouted triumphantly. "If that's not vengeance, what is it? You're blaming Mason for sending you to the pen—and for marrying the woman you had your sights set on, and now you're back to square up with him. You say that's not the truth?"

"Only a part of it—and far as me going to the pen, I was framed, and you damn sure know it!"

"I know how they jury saw it—because I was on that jury," Major stated angrily. "We went by the facts—"

"You went by what Sid Mason wanted you to," Cameron said flatly. "Brand Redmon had a gun in his hand when I shot him. Somebody took it—took the evidence that would have cleared me."

Major, a fairly young man, clean-shaven, and dressed in denim pants, low-heeled jackboots, and cotton work shirt, ran a hand nervously through his blond hair, and brushed at the sweat on his forehead.

"Was no proof of that," he said defensively.

"It's the truth just the same. Sid was behind it all. Had me put away—railroaded they call it up in the pen—

because I was starting to wake folks up around here, make them realize what he was up to."

Wilson's lips parted into a fixed smile. "And just what do you claim Sid Mason's up to?"

"He's fixing to take over the whole valley. You'd see that if you didn't have gold pieces for eyes! He's out to own every acre of land in this part of the country. Hell, he's even boasted about doing it—and he's getting the property in any way he can."

"Mason's buying up land, I'll agree—"

"He's also stealing it, either by paying maybe a tenth of what it's worth, or he's out and out scaring off the folks that own it under threat of—"

"If that's true," Major cut in, "and I'm plenty sure it ain't, why haven't those people you claim have been crooked or run off gone to the marshal about it?"

"Been a couple of families that tried back when I was working to get folks around here to set tight and not give in to Mason. One of the men, Abe Zody, ended up dead. Nobody ever knew who bushwhacked him. The other family, the Conwells, had their team stampeded one morning when they were driving over to talk to the law. A couple of their kids were bad hurt, along with Conwell's missus."

"And you're blaming Sid for that?"

"He was behind it. Maybe he didn't take a hand in the actual stampeding of Conwell's horses, or the bushwhacking of Abe Zody, but he had somebody do it—probably Bear Kugan or the Redmons."

"Which all adds up to why you've come back here—to pick up fighting Sid Mason where you left off—"

"Just what I plan to do—you both might as well know it so's you can go running to Sid with the word. I'm going to drive him out of the country—if it's the last thing I do!"

The banker laughed. "That's probably how it'll be—the last thing you ever do. You think you can do this alone?"

"Expect to have some help. I think folks around here have woke up some during the past three years while I was away, and are seeing that I was right. I figure to get them together, make up a sort of vigilante committee, and put a stop to Mason's gobbling up the few small ranchers and homesteaders that are left, and see if we can't get back some of the property he's swindled or stolen from others."

Aaron Wilson whistled softly. "That's a mighty big chore for one man—specially when he's short on friends."

"For a fact," Major agreed. "It's plenty true when you take a look at the size of Mason and his Muleshoe outfit. Expect there ain't no spread bigger this side of the Panhandle."

"Not as far as I know," Wilson said. "And since we're dealing in truth, what's wrong with Mason taking over all these little two-bit, starve-out ranches and homesteads? The way I see it, it's good for the town. The man spends a lot of money here, and it's cash at the end of the month—all accounts paid in full, and no carrying the bill for month after month—and maybe not even collecting half of the debt when it's due. Ain't that so, George?"

Morgan, silent since the banker and the hardware store man had come in, shrugged. "Yeh, reckon it is."

"And you—all of you—think that's a good thing for the valley?" Cameron persisted.

"Of course it is!" Wilson declared flatly. "Why, this

town could just about exist on the business it will get from Sid Mason!"

"And to hell with the regular folks, that it? They've got no right to their hopes and dreams, or wanting to have their own place where they can bring up their kids, and live the kind of life they'd like? Only Sid Mason has those rights—that what you're claiming?"

Wilson glanced at Major, and then lifting his hands, let them fall to his sides in a gesture of frustration.

"You're not thinking straight, Cameron! I believe being cooped up in the pen for three years has turned you pure loco!"

"That's for dang sure!" Major stated, bobbing his head vigorously. "Him coming back here proves that, but trying to make us swallow that bull about running off Sid for the good of the country—that really shows him up for a looney!".

"And a firebrand along with it," the banker pointed out. "If you're not careful, Cameron, you're going to set this whole valley afire!"

"Maybe," Cameron replied calmly, "that's what it needs to wake it up." He turned to Morgan. "What about those supplies?"

Morgan swiped at the shine on his face with a red bandanna handkerchief and nodded slightly.

"Expect I can string along with you for a little while if—"

Aaron Wilson was shaking his head, denoting his disapproval. Pete Major swore.

"If what?" Cameron asked.

"If it ain't too much. You got a list?"

Cameron handed over the slip of paper he'd made out earlier while at Ketty Griffin's detailing the items he felt would be needed—mostly food, cooking utensils, a couple of blankets.

"Be needing some lumber and the like, I figure, but I don't know just what and how much until I've had a look at my place."

"Talk to Major about that," Morgan said bluntly. "I've got out of building supplies."

"You won't get a nickel's worth of anything from me," the hardware store man said quickly.

Cameron considered him with amusement. "Can see you know which side of your bread the butter's on."

"Why not? I'd be a damn fool to mess up my own nest. I've got more cash in the bank now from my business than I've ever had—thanks to Sid Mason and his trade. Sure don't aim to hurt myself some by favoring a jackleg troublemaker like you."

Cameron's features darkened, and his wide shoulders came up to form a straight line. He seemed about to make a reply, but after giving it a second thought, let the matter slide.

"Like to ask you one question, Major—you, too, Wilson; how many new people have moved into the valley since Mason and his bunch started running loose, having their way?"

The banker frowned, loosening the neckband of his shirt with a forefinger. "Well, right off I can't think of anybody just now. What's that got to do with what we're talking about?"

"Proves what I've been trying to make folks like you see. Mason's killed off the valley as far as it ever growing is concerned. Folks won't move in—either to ranch or farm, or go into some kind of business. The word's got around about Mason and his gun hands, and nobody wants to settle here now. Way it's going Red Rock Valley is going to end up one big ranch—his."

"I hardly think that's so," Wilson said stiffly. "You're making things out worse than they can ever be."

"Not from what I've heard since I got back. There are fewer small ranches than there were three years ago. Same goes for homesteads—and that tots up to just one thing: Mason's been real busy while I was gone. I reckon if he could've made that ten-year sentence he got that judge to give me stick, he would have swallowed up the whole valley and turned it into a part of Muleshoe by the time I got back."

Aaron Wilson remained silent. Outside the afternoon's hush was broken by the steady thud of a loping horse as a rider passed along the street, and over in the direction of the church someone was practicing on a piano, the notes faint and tentative.

"Just too damn bad you ever got out," Pete Major said, and then abruptly halted what else he was about to say when Cameron whirled to face him.

"Pete, we were friends once, and only that keeps me from knocking talk like that back down your throat! But I'm getting plenty tired of it, and my patience is running short. I'm warning you now—best you watch your step!"

Major had fallen back a step, his features taut and with a whiteness around the mouth. Aaron Wilson shook his head.

"Was hoping we could talk this out without any violence, Cameron. Pete's just worried like everybody else around here about the trouble you seem bent on stirring up. What would it take to get you to move on, get out of the valley and stay out?"

Cameron laughed. "Don't waste your time thinking about

that, Wilson. You or nobody else's got that kind of money! I've come back to fix up my place as much as I can, get back the two hundred steers Mason stole from me, hire myself a crew, and start ranching again—and while I'm doing that I'll be talking to the rest of the ranchers and farmers, getting them to make a stand with me against Mason."

"Now, where do you think you'll get a crew?" Aaron Wilson asked. "You won't find any men in Wolf Springs who'll sign up to fight Muleshoe—and that's what it will amount to."

"I'll get one—probably over in Silver City where I'll be buying my supplies from now on. Happens I know—"

"Here's your stuff," George Morgan broke in, laying a half-filled flour sack and a folded blanket on the counter. "Best I can do for you."

Cameron grasped the sack by its neck, and hung it and the blanket over a shoulder. "How much do I owe you?"

Morgan frowned, brushed at his lips. "Thought you was wanting credit—"

"Seeing where you stand I changed my mind," Cameron said, producing his roll of currency. "How much?"

"Five dollars'll cover it. If I'd known—"

Cameron laid the necessary amount on the counter. "Would've liked to do business with you again, George, like in the old days," he said, "but looks like I'll be better off making the half-day ride to Silver City. When I get back my cattle—"

"Which you can't prove you own," Major observed.

"No problem there. Made a point of telling a U.S. deputy marshal about my herd before I was put away, asked them to appoint somebody to sell it off and bank the money for me. It was never done. So far as the law's concerned my stock is still out there on my land, running loose. If the steers ain't there, then we'll find them in Mason's herd because there's nobody else around to take them."

Turning, sack and blanket over his shoulder, Cameron started for the door. Midway he halted, facing the banker and Pete Major.

"Just thought I'd better warn you—if any of Mason's bunch try ambushing me on the way to Silver City, I'll know where they got the word that I was making the trip—and I'll come looking for you!"

"Now, hold on just a damned minute!" Wilson shouted angrily. "You can't—"

"And something else, I'm heading for Charlie Sweeney's livery stable to get myself a horse. Don't follow me. I don't want either one of you standing around throwing looks at Charlie while I'm trying to deal him out of something to ride. Hear?"

Waiting until both the banker and the hardware store owner had nodded, indicating their understanding, Cameron continued on to the doorway, and out onto the littered landing. Pausing there for a brief glance along the empty street, he then descended the steps and struck for the livery stable, the last building in the row.

He probably had talked far too much, Cameron realized, as again wary of the bushwhacker, he strode toward Sweeney's. But everything he'd said had been bottled up inside him for so long that it had to come out, and he was glad that Aaron Wilson was one of those who had heard it; the banker had always been a strong admirer of Sid Mason and to him the owner of Muleshoe could do no wrong.

One thing was certain, he thought grimly, he could

count on Sid Mason being fully informed of what had been said, and of his plans to rebuild his place—the J-Bar-C. Perhaps it would have been better to remain close-mouthed about it, allow himself to get the initial, necessary work done, and have a crew on hand before Mason was aware of what was going on.

But thinking it over, John reckoned it wouldn't have worked out that way. Sid Mason would have word of his activities almost as soon as he began to work, carried to the rancher either by one of his Muleshoe riders or some toadying acquaintance hoping to make points. Cameron reckoned it didn't matter much anyway; he had small hope of making a go of the J-Bar-C, and intended to use it only as a base from which to carry on his campaign against Mason—vegeance, Aaron Wilson had called it.

It wasn't vengeance, Cameron assured himself. If that was all it amounted to he could settle the matter quickly simply by hunting up Mason, forcing him into a gunfight, and killing him. No, hate perhaps, but not vengeance. What he had set himself to do was break Mason's hold on the valley, and drive him out.

Killing Muleshoe's owner was a last resort, something that would occur only if the rancher chose to make a stand and shoot it out. Cameron's step slowed while his narrowed glance continued to switch back and forth along the street in a constant search for danger, noting the stiff, hostile looks on the faces of those who watched him pass. The livery stable was to his left, and now immediately ahead. Veering his course, he approached the wide, open doorway and entered.

Halting just inside, reveling briefly in the coolness and the good rank odors of fresh hay, horses, and leather that filled the sprawling structure, Cameron laid the blanket and sack of grub on a nearby bench, and pulled off his hat.

"Charlie!" he called, running fingers through his damp, dark hair.

"In here—"

The response had come from the small office in the forward corner of the building where a window overlooked the street. The stableman had undoubtedly seen him coming, but had made no effort to meet and welcome him. Cameron shrugged. It was increasingly clear that Sid Mason had broadened his grip on the Red Rock Valley country in the past three years to the point where, in effect, he now owned it. Crossing the runway, Cameron stepped into Sweeney's office, small and filled with trapped heat.

"Seen you coming," the stableman said. A squat, overall-clad man with a beet red face, ragged whiskers, and dwindling hair, he was fanning himself with a lath-handled square of cardboard.

"Sure appreciate your welcome," Cameron replied dryly. "Need a horse. You willing to do some trading, or are you scared to deal with me, too?"

Sweeney shifted the cud in his mouth, and spat into a nearby bucket filled with sand. "I reckon you're talking about Sid Mason," he said, getting to his feet.

"I am—"

"Well, I stay out of his way, and he stays out of mine—that's how we get along. And far as business goes, ain't nobody telling me how to run mine."

"Pleasure to hear that. You've got my saddle and bridle around somewhere—leastwise you never sent word to me that you'd sold them."

"They're here," Sweeney said, jerking a thumb in the

direction of a door in the opposite wall—one that led into a tack room, Cameron recalled. "You was wanting too much money for them. Was a couple or three fellows looked your outfit over, but backed off when I told them what you was asking for them. You want them now?"

Cameron's mouth tightened. Charlie Sweeney, a man he'd known for the past ten years, and at whose home he had been a welcome guest, had failed to extend a greeting, much less a welcome. But, he reckoned, he should expect it.

"No, aiming to do some swapping with them," he said.

"Swapping?" Sweeney echoed. "Meaning what?"

"I need a horse. I'm short on cash so I'm looking to trade my saddle, bridle, blanket—the whole works—for something I can ride."

"You figure to pay some boot?" Sweeney asked, his manner strictly business.

"Damn little, if any. That's a hundred-dollar saddle. Rest of the outfit's worth at least another fifty."

"Maybe," the stableman said skeptically. "Sure ain't run across nobody that's willing to go that high."

"Could be," Cameron said, "maybe the right fellow just hasn't come along yet."

He was relieved to learn that Sweeney still had the hull, a double-rigged, scrolled, and silver-decorated affair that had cost him plenty in Wichita the time he'd gone there to deliver a prisoner for the marshal. He'd gotten himself a bit liquored up, and blown his entire poke on the saddle and a matching bridle. He had cursed himself for it the following day, but now he was glad he'd fallen victim to the saddler's glib tongue, using the gear to trade for a horse would save him from using what cash he had.

"You willing to take in my outfit on something I can ride?"

"Depends," Sweeney said with the caution of a longtime horse trader. "I've got a little mare back there. Sort of old, but—"

"Forget the mare, Charlie. I need something that'll stand up under hard use. Just because they had me locked up in the pen for three years doesn't mean I've forgot all I know about horses."

Sweeney scrubbed at his stubble of whiskers. "Well, you can take a look at what I've got out back," he said. Moving past Cameron, he turned into the runway and struck for the rear of the stable.

There were only three horses in the corral, the mare—a drooping worn-out gray—a black that had one blue eye, and a small but tough-appearing buckskin gelding.

Without comment Cameron entered the enclosure and, arms wide, herded the buckskin into a corner where he checked him over closely. He couldn't expect much for what he was willing to pay, but on the other hand it would be foolish to waste what he did have to trade on an animal that had seen its best days.

"What's wrong with him?" he asked then, stepping back and pointing at the buckskin.

"There ain't nothing wrong with him!" Sweeney replied indignantly, coming into the corral.

"There's scars on his left front leg like maybe he was having forging trouble. Teeth says he's getting close to ten years old."

"He ain't a day over seven—and I sure ain't ever seen him hitting hisself none."

"Well, take a look for yourself," Cameron said, pointing to the area above the horse's left front hoof where the toe of the corresponding hind foot had struck. "Not too happy with a buckskin, anyway. Heard it said they sunburn mighty easy."

"Ain't nothing to that!" Sweeney declared. "I'll take a buckskin to a black seven days in the week."

"That so? How about his wind? He ain't been broke, has he? Sounds to me like I can hear a bit of wheezing, or maybe it's a touch of the heaves—"

"Damn it to hell, Cameron, if you—"

"Got white forelegs, too, and that's not good. Should be black, same as his mane and tail. Means he's got lord only knows what kind of a blood mix. Could be a real good animal, or a poor one with no bottom or wind."

Sweeney scrubbed irritably at his jaw again. "To hear you talk the gelding ain't worth nothing at all!"

"Sure could be, Charlie," Cameron said, looking around, "but seems he's the best you've got to sell. I'll trade you my saddle for him, and some kind of an old hull and blanket to use—"

"Yeh, I reckon you would! Now, I'll tell you what I'll do. I'll swap him for your saddle, bridle, and some boot."

Cameron turned away, gazed thoughtfully at the mare and the black, both standing slack-hipped and head down in the blazing sun.

"I'm wondering if I couldn't do better somewheres else," he said. "Going to have to make a trip to Silver City. Just might be smart to hold off and see what I can work out over there."

"How you going to get there? Long walk—"

"Lady friend of mine can do some borrowing for me, and—"

"What'll you give for the buckskin?" Sweeney cut in wearily. "Let's cut out this jockeying around, and get down to business. I'm willing to sell him, you're willing to buy. Let's strike a bargain."

"Fair enough," Cameron agreed. "I'm ready to trade my gear, the whole kit and kaboodle—saddle, bridle, blanket, and saddlebags—for the buckskin and tack of some kind that I can use on him. Don't have to be real good, just something I can use till I get my ranch to going."

"Well, I expect I can fix you up there. Was a cowhand sold me his whole rigging, even got a canteen and a rifle boot with it. Now, you fork over twenty dollars and the buckskin and the rigging's yours."

Cameron gave the offer thought. It wasn't exactly the kind of trade he'd consider a good one, but he needed a horse and gear, and he doubted he could do any better elsewhere. Besides, if he backed off it meant he'd have to lug his tack off to where he could try and strike up another trade.

"Let me see that cowhand's outfit," he said, coming to a decision.

Sweeney doubled back into the livery barn and turned into the first stall at the end of the runway. Pointing to a worn saddle with a bridle hanging from it that had been tossed into the manger, he said, "That's it."

The leather of the reins was dry-cracked, and the bridle was little more than a hackamore; the blanket was a moth-eaten old Indian rug, and while it had several holes, was usable. The hull itself was not too bad, both the horn and the cantle being firm, and the stirrup leather showing wear but still strong.

"Don't figure it's all I ought to get for my gear," Cameron said, taking hold of the saddle and lifting it with its accompanying equipment out of the manger, "but I'll

trade—long as I've got your word that there's nothing
wrong with the horse."

Sweeney bobbed reassuringly. "I ain't about to palm
off no ringer on you, John. Do want to say this, he's a
mite gun-shy, but not enough to give you no trouble."

Cameron shook his head. "You sure there ain't a few
other drawbacks you ought to tell me about?"

"Nope, you got my word."

"All right. You get the papers made out while I go
saddle up."

"Won't take me but a couple of minutes, more or less,"
Sweeney said, and turned back into the runway for his
office as Cameron, saddle and other equipment over his
shoulder, started back to the corral.

A half hour later Cameron was astride the buckskin
heading out of the settlement for his ranch—or what
remained of it. The gelding appeared to be a fair horse,
at least so far, and Cameron reckoned he hadn't done so
badly after all. Important thing was that he had conserved
his cash—and cash money was something he'd need if he
was to hire a crew and do his trading in distant Silver
City.

But he'd take it one day at a time, let matters shape up
as they willed. Good thing about it all was that he was
home again, that Ketty Griffin still cared for him, and he
was once more in the saddle. Things couldn't be much
better than that.

CHAPTER 4

~~~~~~

Ketty stood in the doorway of her house and watched John Cameron move off down the path for the street. He was a high, square-shouldered shape in the afternoon sunlight, and the thought occurred to her that he always carried himself well regardless of conditions or his state of mind.

She had hated to see him go, to see their day end. It had been wonderful spending the hours with him, recalling the good times they'd had, the happy things they had done before change—in the form of Darcy Bellamy—had come into their lives.

They had laughed as they remembered some of their experiences, and Ketty had cried a bit now and then, at which moments Cameron had taken her into his arms, and with a gentleness that belied his muscular strength, comforted her. On the other hand she had caught a glimpse of the bitterness that lay deep within him, and done her best to allay it, but with little success, she feared.

An intense hatred was smoldering inside him, a living force that needed only proper time and conditions to burst into violent, roaring flame. And that moment would come when he encountered Sid Mason face to face and had it out with him. There could be no other answer to the determination that possessed him like an all-consuming disease. He had it fixed in his mind that Mason was the ruination of his beloved Red Rock Valley—which he surely was—and had taken it upon himself to put an end to such.

He would let nothing else, not his love and need for her of which Ketty was now certain, or his hope to one day have a fine ranch in the valley, stand in the way of his obsession. And while she knew she was everything to him Ketty was acutely aware that she could be sacrificed should she make any effort to dissuade him from his avowed purpose.

Cameron actually frightened her a little. He had changed from a somewhat easygoing man to one of grim intensity, but as the afternoon had worn on, he had loosened up some and become at least a shadow of his old self. He had assured her that he would return after he'd taken care of some necessary business and had a look at what remained of his J-Bar-C ranch.

Ketty had felt a twinge of fear as she watched John Cameron turn into the street and head for George Morgan's General Store. He was defying danger—death in fact— when he moved about in the open. She had called that to his attention as he was preparing to leave, but he had shrugged and said that he wouldn't hide in the shadows, that he had no time for such.

His attitude had sent a tremor of fear through her for she was fully aware of the ruthless ways of Sid Mason and the men who worked for him. That John Cameron knew such only made it all the more frightening to her since he accepted that knowledge with an indifference which indicated he was willing to confront whatever came his way with no qualms or reservations.

The thought of losing him to death brought a stillness to her heart. She had loved him almost from the minute she'd arrived in Wolf Springs, over five years ago, a young girl sick of the drudgery of farm life, and seeking a new and better world.

John Cameron had recognized her for what she was, and acting as deputy town marshal at the time, had taken her under his wing, seen to it that she had a decent place to stay, and found her a job with Tom Briscoe at the High Ridge Saloon & Restaurant. /

He'd made it clear to Briscoe that she was not to be considered one of the ordinary saloon women granting favors for pay to the men who patronized the place, but was to work as a calico girl, the name applied to the women who waited on tables serving drinks and food. Briscoe, a friend of Cameron's, had complied, and she had fared well in the High Ridge, even after Briscoe had been killed by a gambler during an argument over cards.

The new owner, Harry Kingman, had honored the agreement existing between Cameron and Briscoe, and had further shown his appreciation of Ketty's good work by putting her in charge of the restaurant part of the saloon. She and John Cameron had become closer by then, and there was talk of marriage which faded and died out not long after Darcy Bellamy had arrived in town from somewhere back East to live with her father and help him in his business.

Ketty's relationship with John Cameron had deteriorated rapidly after that, and within a short time Darcy had let it be known that she and John Cameron were to be married. Only a day or so after that the trouble between Cameron and Sid Mason, which had been intensifying, came to a head when Cameron was forced to kill Brand Redmon, one of Mason's riders. A trial quickly followed which resulted in John being sent off to prison.

Her love for John Cameron had never wavered during all those months, and there was always the belief that he would come back to her one day—which was just what he had done. His feelings for her were stronger than ever, Ketty was certain, and she did her best to weld him to her by returning his love. But that was possible only up to a point; he'd not resume any sort of normal life with serious intentions toward her until he had accomplished what he had vowed to do.

Sighing, Ketty turned away from the door. John Cameron was no longer in sight; she might as well get ready to go to work. Crossing to the bed, she removed the robe she was wearing and drew on the yellow dress. After a moment Ketty took it off, changing her mind about using it since it was the one John had first seen her in when he arrived, and she now had a special feeling for the garment.

Drawing aside the curtain that hung over the opening in the wardrobe, she placed the yellow dress on a hanger and selected a tan skirt which she would complement with a white shirtwaist. Such would be much more sensible in the High Ridge.

A knock at the door brought Ketty hurriedly around, fear clutching at her throat. But that quickly dissipated, and was replaced by a frown. Through the screen she could see Darcy, and beyond her the familiar red-wheeled buggy and sorrel horse she drove. Resentment and anger stirred through Ketty. Why did Darcy Mason have to show up? What right did she have to intrude on this day of happiness?

"Just a moment," she called when Darcy repeated her knocking.

Finishing dressing, Ketty moved to the door, released the hook, and stepped out onto the landing. Somehow she didn't relish the thought of asking Darcy into the house.

"Yes?"

Darcy, clad in a dove-gray silk dress that fit her figure very well, glanced toward the street, and then again faced Ketty.

"I—I expect you're wondering why I'm here," she began hesitantly.

Ketty nodded. "It's the first time since you brought me John's gun—"

"Is—is he here?" Darcy broke in.

"No."

Darcy dabbed at her lips with a handkerchief, again looked off in the direction of the street. "But he was," she said, comimg back around. "I know that. How is he?"

The question came in a quick rush of words. Ketty shrugged, leaning back against the doorframe. Resentment was building steadily within her.

"He's well enough after three years in the pen."

"Did being there change him much?"

She could tell Darcy that John Cameron was over at the General Store, and that she could go see for herself, but she was damned if she'd do it! Darcy was out of John's life, and that was the way she wanted it to stay.

"No, if anything he's stronger—more of a man than he ever was. There was a lot of hard work—"

"How does he seem? Did he—"

"Ask about you. That what you're getting at?"

Darcy again brushed at her full lips, straightened her collar. She was pretty, Ketty supposed, in a doll-like way. She had a wealth of honey-colored hair, large brown eyes, and what could be considered a flawless skin. It was not hard to see how she had captivated John Cameron, and then after he was gone and out of the picture, set her cap for, and gotten, wealthy Sid Mason.

"Yes, I guess I am."

"Well, he didn't—not exactly. We talked about a lot of things, and your name came up. It shouldn't matter to you anyway, Darcy. You've made yourself another life—leave John Cameron out of it."

"Yes, I know—and I'm trying," Darcy said in a falling voice. "I won't do anything to come between you and him, it's just that I had to know."

"He'll be all right. Always was a man who could take care of himself. I'm sure he still can."

Darcy nodded. Then, "Sid knows he's back, and he's told Bear Kugan and some of the others to get ready for trouble."

"Was it one of them who tried to shoot him right after he got off the stage?"

"I don't know," Darcy replied, frowning. "I hadn't heard about that. Was John hit?"

"No. He saw whoever it was raise his gun, and jumped to one side. When he got to where the shot came from there was nobody there."

Tears filled Darcy Mason's eyes. "Oh, it's all so terrible!

I wish he'd never come back! It can only end with him getting killed!"

"It could be your husband that dies," Ketty observed coolly. "Best you worry about him. I'll look after John Cameron."

Darcy murmured, "Of course," as that bit of practical advice reached her. "Will you be marrying him?" she added.

"Soon, I think," Ketty answered, stretching the fact a trifle, and taking joy in seeing Darcy flinch slightly.

It was not an out-and-out bold lie; she and John had discussed marriage, and he had intimated that as soon as things had settled down, and the valley was no longer being crushed underfoot by Mason, they would make plans. Personally, she had told Cameron, she would prefer not to wait; she wanted to share every minute with him, good or bad, dangerous or otherwise, but he maintained such was unfair to her, and that it was only realistic to hold off.

"Congratulations," Darcy said in a low voice. "I'm sure you'll be very happy."

"I'll see to it," Ketty stated. "I understand John—know what he likes and wants. I intend to do all I can to help him."

Once again Darcy glanced toward the street. Then, "He can't fight Sid and win. If you love him as much as you say, you'll talk him out of this, this foolishness about driving Sid out of the valley. One of the men, Quint Redmon, heard him tell the marshal that was what he'd come back here to do."

"I'll stand by John in whatever he wants to do. Maybe I won't agree, but I'll back him just the same."

"Even if it's wrong—a mistake?"

"No matter what. I think that's what loving a man's all about—standing by him, and believing in him no matter how it may come out. I don't suppose that makes any sense to you."

"I'm not sure that it does—"

"If it did," Ketty said with a fine edge to her voice, "you'd probably be with him today. But you turned your back on him when he needed you most."

"I—I did what I thought best—"

"I suppose," Ketty said, reaching for the handle of the screen door, an indication that the conversation was over. "But that's all behind us now. John has come back to me and I intend to hold him."

"I understand—and in something like this I know we never get a second chance," Darcy said, turning to leave. She paused. "Can I ask a favor?"

Wary, Ketty shrugged. "Depends. We have nothing in common, Mrs. Mason, so I hardly see how I can be in a position to do you a favor."

Darcy Mason smiled wryly at the formality Ketty's tone had adopted. "I don't blame you for hating me, and—"

"I don't hate you—I hate what you did to John, and what you put him through."

And could again, Ketty was thinking. She was not all that certain, despite all her self-confidence, that John Cameron had gotten Darcy out of his system even though he insisted that everything was over between them. In truth, Ketty looked forward to the time when they would meet, accidentally or otherwise, with considerable apprehension.

"I just wanted you to tell him that I asked about him—that I'm glad he's well and out of that prison."

Ketty rode out a long minute, and then a cool, enig-
matic smile parted her lips. "Good-bye, Mrs. Mason,"
she said quietly, and opening the door turned back into
the house.

CHAPTER 5

Cameron followed the dusty road leading west out of town, and thus bore directly into the late afternoon sun. But he did not find it disagreeable; to the contrary, the feel of a horse between his legs and the comforting pressure of a gun against his hip had a reassuring effect upon him, filling him with a sort of ease and contentment.

Thoughts were crowding his mind, as they will do when a man rides solitarily across a vast, quiet land of rolling hills and plains, and it came to John Cameron that in a valley where he once could have called every man friend, he now was, except for Ketty Griffin, entirely alone—and she, he was forced to admit, did not fully understand why he felt he must do what he planned.

The same went, of course, for George Morgan and Charlie Sweeney—and all the others with whom he had once been close. He supposed he shouldn't blame them for their attitude; it was clear they feared retribution, in one form or another, from Sid Mason and his hired toughs if they showed any indication of welcoming and assisting him. And, too, they most likely felt, as banker Aaron Wilson did, that mighty Muleshoe's business came ahead of friendship.

Cameron had hoped to find some degree of support in his effort to break Sid Mason's stranglehold on Red Rock Valley, but so far there had been no sign of such other than Ketty, which stirred him deeply, but actually counted for little; he needed the kind of help that sat a saddle and would use a gun when necessary.

He'd not find such among those who once professed to be his friends, that was now certain; he could only hope to recruit from the homesteaders and ranchers who had lost to Mason, or were about to, and press into service the three or four men he intended to hire as a crew to assist him in recovering his steers from Muleshoe, and putting the ranch back into some semblance of working order.

It was necessary that it be done—the reconstruction of the J-Bar-C and the recovering of the stock appropriated from him by Mason after the rancher had successfully and effectively disposed of him, for in many minds there would exist doubt. What could he hope to accomplish against such odds, they would wonder. Broke, friendless, with everyone turned against him, what chance did he have of winning?

The reason for such was perfectly clear in John Cameron's mind; by making an effort to rebuild his ranch, and reclaiming his stock, which meant riding onto Muleshoe range and boldly driving the steers back onto his own land, he would prove that Muleshoe could be defied— that Sid Mason was not invincible after all—and thereby build hope in the hearts of those about to be crushed by the rancher, or those who had already felt his heel.

And equally effective insofar as he was concerned,

such would be tantamount to s
the face, causing him to declare
would be quickly brought to a hea
would not be forced to go up aga
Muleshoe gunmen alone; by that time
whom he was making a stand would ha
dom of his efforts and rallied to his side.

From beneath the down-slanted brim of
eron let his gaze slide over the familiar lands
ing before him. The road followed a course
edge of the low, brushy swells, and across gras
gray-green now from summer's heat—which was
expected at that time of year. But the land wa
forsaken; now and then doves and other birds flew in
out of the junipers and scrub oaks that dotted the are
and twice he saw deer bound off in alarm at the passage.

In the long distance the peaks and ridges of the Navajo
Mountains were dark-shadowed lifts and falls as canyons
and saddles alternately laced their slopes; and when a
square-edge hogback marched past one of the higher
crags light glinted off its side like water mirroring the
sun.

Remembering then, with a sudden clarity, John Cameron swung his glance to the far northern end of the
towering hills where a stone shelf formed a balcony that
overlooked a broad green valley.

It was not visible to him from so great a distance, but
he recalled well the day he and Darcy Bellamy had
ridden to that point and enjoyed a picnic—just the two of
them, alone, in a world so vast that it was totally unaware
of their presence. They had talked at length about the
many things they would do in the days to come, and
made great plans for the future as a man and woman

...d brought his
...the brushy
...nnumera-
...at Shelf
...ned to
...came

...od, he thought,
...back pastures should
...Sid Mason had not taken
...n herds—and where his graze
...ajos, the range should be excellent.
...Cameron eased back in the saddle, let
...acken to slow the buckskin, which had proved
...e a comfortable, loping gait, and looked to his
...ight.

In that general direction lay his spread, the J-Bar-C. It began just this side of Texhama Creek, and ran the full distance to the mountains. Immediately to the south were the Claude Ivey and Tom Lear ranches, still holdouts according to Ketty, and on beyond them came the eight or ten homesteads and small ranches that Mason had acquired.

To his north was Lige Davidson's Rocking D outfit, as large as his own, bordered on both north and east by Muleshoe, which now engulfed almost all of the valley.

The country was a cattleman's dream; ample grass, good, constant water, and not too distant hills rearing their protective bulk the entire width of the valley to shut off the hard winter snows and freezing winds that came down from farther north. And Sid Mason wanted it all—

had made it plain that it eventually would be his. Like many ranchers of similar stature there was no end to his greed once he had tasted growth and known success; such men were never satisfied, always desired more.

Cameron reached the crest of the flint-rock hill that marked his southeastern boundary, and had his first look in three years of the J-Bar-C. There was no fence—never had been; there was only the ragged, surfaced mound to serve as a marker, just as piles of stones at the three other corners indicated the limits of his property. A feeling of pride stirred through Cameron as he sat there gazing out over the land—his land.

This was his—his alone, and not anyone on earth would ever take it from him unless he killed him first. He'd never succumb to Sid Mason's efforts to make him sign over what was his as had many others; if by doing so he could buy his way out of hell, he'd still refuse. Everything might now be gone—friends, his part-time job as a deputy marshal, buildings that he had so painstakingly built—but the land was still there patiently awaiting his return. As long as there was breath in his body he'd never surrender it.

Feeling curiously subdued, but now more convinced than ever of the need to be on the alert for another bushwhacking attempt, Cameron rode down the slight grade, allowing his narrowed eyes to run along the familiar contours of the ranch visible from that point.

The sky was a great bowl of deep blue bending overhead, and Texhama Creek was a clear, sparkling ribbon meandering along the valley's floor. The air was fresh, although still hot, and the smell of rabbit brush, juniper, bee plant, wild timothy, and other growth was strong in his nostrils. Leaning back on the buckskin, Cameron sucked in his fill of it all—a man coming home—and when at last he reached the faint, twin trails left by the wheels of his wagon long ago, he cut away from the main road which continued on to Davidson's on the right, Claude Ivey, and others, to the left, and followed it onto his property. There he halted the buckskin and dismounted.

Many times at night in the overcrowded cell at the penitentiary, after the day's brutal labor was over, he had lived this very moment. On countless occasions John Cameron had pictured what it would be like to again ride down the slope and enter the world that was his by right of hard-won ownership.

He had a fleeting urge to bend over, scoop up a double handful of the dry, brown soil, and hold it tight. But he grinned off that bit of sentimental nonsense and merely stood there, wholly still, with the sun showering down upon him and the sound of a meadowlark whistling cheerily off in the distance filling his ears. In those almost solemn, rapt moments a measure of the deep bitterness that lay within him passed from his being, and he was free of all the dark memories, grim threats, and recollections of savage violence, and he was as he had once been, a man with a soul at peace.

After a time he climbed back into the saddle, and still possessed by a quiet mood, raised the head of the buckskin, reluctant to forsake the grass he was enjoying, and continued slowly along the dim lanes.

When he reached the banks of the Texhama a change came over him abruptly, for here he saw the first signs of Sid Mason's further visitations. The plank bridge across the creek was gone, parts of it split and rotting, scattered along the edges of the stream, other pieces lying waterlogged below its surface. The buttresses—the rocks for which he'd hauled in with such backbreaking labor from the distant Navajos—were gone entirely.

Wading the horse through the knee-deep water to the opposite bank, Cameron resumed the trail, coming next to the tall posts from which his identifying sign had hung from a crossbeam. It had been a short plank upon which he had burned his J-BAR-C brand, suspending it by two lengths of chain to denote his ownership. Now it was a splintered, illegible bit of debris riddled with bullet holes dangling lifelessly by one chain.

He had erected his buildings in a small hollow where two giant cottonwoods had created an island of shade. They stood full-leafed and spreading, inviting him now as they had numberless times in the past to pause and rest in the coolness of their shadows. He was thankful they had escaped the vandalistic attention of Mason's crew.

They alone had been overlooked, however. The main house, put together by him board by board, and consisting of a living room, kitchen, sleeping quarters, and a full-width porch running across its front, was a charred, blackened ghost of what it had been. What furniture he'd had was gone, either burned or carried off. Only the four-hole stove upon which he had relied for both heat and cooking remained; it lay prostrate on its side, one leg missing, and the pipe a disjointed trail nearby.

A sullen fury now glowing within him, Cameron moved on. The well pump which had stood near the back door of the house was canted drunkenly, undoubtedly drawn to such an awkward angle by the rope of some rider in a playful mood. Beyond it, all that marked the locations of the toolshed and other minor structures were wind-blown squares of ashes along which weeds and grass had begun to grow, as if hopeful of hiding the ugly scars.

The bunkhouse, built of sod, was the sole survivor of the vandalism. Cameron, anger now a seething flame inside him, came off the buckskin gelding, and ground-reining him, crossed slowly to the low-roofed, squat-looking structure. The door hung from a single leather hinge, and the glass of the two windows—once only ragged, round holes that he had squared and then installed wooden frames—had been methodically punched out. The walls, and the dirt roof, thankfully, were still intact.

Entering, Cameron found the bunks ripped from their moorings and the small, pot-bellied heating stove, held prisoner by its flue, standing drunkenly on one leg. The floor nearby was scarred by a fire that had been built on the pine planks. Fortunately it had not burned for long and damage was not extensive. He had hoped, and was finding it to be true, the bunkhouse had suffered no great damage and could be made livable. Relieved, and anger dwindling somewhat, he returned to the yard.

The buckskin was grazing over by the sharply canted hitch rack. Unsaddling the animal and slipping the bit, Cameron led him into the shade of the cottonwood trees and there picketed him. Turning then, he began a search among the ruins for any tools that might be serviceable; anything that could be salvaged and used meant that much less cash he would have to spend.

He found an axhead in the ashes of the storeroom, and a hammer with its handle half gone lying behind the bunkhouse where it had been thrown. Other than those two items he discovered nothing with which he could work, and taking the hammer, he returned to the bunkhouse where he began to put in order as much as possible.

The bunks were fairly easy to repair and restore to their places along the walls. The straw ticks Cameron carried out into the sunlight, draping them over convenient clumps of brush and dusting them thoroughly with a length of wood. The heating stove he pushed into a corner, and by use of a drag, managed to bring the cookstove from the remains of the ranch house and set it up in its new quarters by using flat rocks to replace the missing leg. There was plenty of pipe to connect it to the flue, and while the affair trembled a bit when he walked near, it would serve the purpose. There was no broom available, but Cameron located a partially burned blanket, and wrapping it about the end of a stick, brushed down the walls and dusted off the shelves, after which he placed upon them the small stock of groceries he'd gotten from George Morgan.

Poking about in the blackened rubble of the kitchen, Cameron found a frying pan, several heat-twisted but usable spoons, forks and knives, a cup, and a lard bucket which showed little effects from the flames, likely having been tossed into the fire when it was all but burned out.

Carrying them to the pump with the hope that the pipe had not been rusted through or broken, he gave it a few tentative strokes. It gave forth nothing but harsh, grating noises when he worked the handle, and after a bit, soaking wet from sweat, he took the lard bucket down to the creek, filling it with water. Returning, he tried priming the pump. At first the screeching from its interior continued, but shortly under the continual inducement from the lard bucket, water gushed from the spout. Cameron pumped steadily until the water came through clear, and the shallow sump nearby was filled for the buckskin's use. Once there had been a trough there, but it was gone now.

It was near sundown by the time John Cameron had finished his first spate of repairs. There was still much to be done, but it was a start. He had a place to eat, to sleep, and be out of the open in the event of bad weather. Next would come a bit more rebuilding; there was need for a corral with a shelter off one end for the horses.

The sod bunkhouse, which was to serve as living quarters for himself and crew, would need to be improved against the not too distant day when winter would set in. He paused on that thought. Perhaps he was looking too far ahead; it could work out there'd be no need to prepare for winter—or for even a week from that day. Cameron shrugged off the dark possibility. He wasn't dead yet, and already Sid Mason had learned that he was hard to get rid of.

Mopping at the sweat on his forehead, aware of his soaked clothing, Cameron felt a weariness overtake him. It had been a long day, and despite the several restful, pleasant hours he'd spent with Ketty Griffin, he was bone-tired—although far from hungry, thanks to the fine meal she had set before him.

The logical thing to do next, he reckoned—since he had done all of the repairing he could with the tools and materials on hand—was go into town and see what he could do about hiring on a crew. Perhaps some of the men who had worked for him before he was sent away were still around and willing to sign on. Aaron Wilson, or maybe it was Pete Major, had warned him he'd find no takers to his offer of work in Wolf Springs. Such was likely, but he'd prefer to see for himself.

Dragging the door to the bunkhouse closed, Cameron crossed to the buckskin, saddled and bitted him, and then with the first stir of an evening breeze touching him, mounted and struck out for the settlement.

CHAPTER 6

A warm, amber hush lay over the hills and flats as John Cameron rode toward town. It occurred to him as the buckskin jogged steadily along that he had all but forgotten how beautiful a sunset could be, and despite the possibility of a Muleshoe ambush, he continually turned his attention to the blaze in the west.

The sky beyond the craggy mountains, which were now a deep purple, was filled with a yellow glow. Spraying upward were fingers of red that grew progressively paler as they reached higher into the heavens. But even as he watched the colors changed; the yellow banked along the horizon became purest gold, and the streamers of red became salmon, and then shafts of orange edged with violets and blues.

He had never tired of the sight, or of the miracle of sunrise, or of the rugged grandeur of the country itself. It was all a deep-seated part of him, and he supposed, when he thought about it, the reason for his stubborn determination to let no man alter any of it.

A sudden flare of alarm raced through him, sending his hand dropping onto the butt of the pistol on his hip. Abrupt, further motion in a dense stand of Apache plume drew his eyes. He drew the buckskin gelding to a halt, and weapon out and ready, he waited. Moments later a lone steer bolted into view and loped off into the gathering darkness. Cameron grinned, holstering the forty-five as the stray vanished into a brushy draw. The threat of being bushwhacked had turned him jumpy.

He reached the settlement not long after full dark had closed in. Stores along the street had lit their lamps, and the windows of the homes scattered about over the surrounding area were squares of yellow light. There was no one abroad at that moment, but there were a dozen or so horses tethered to the hitch racks fronting the High Ridge and the town's only other saloon, the Cottonwood.

Guiding the buckskin into the alternate rack at the side of the High Ridge where there were but three mounts waiting, Cameron swung down, secured the gelding to the rail, and made his way to the rear door of the establishment. Surprised to find it locked, Cameron dropped back, circled the building, and entered through the front.

The night's activities were already in full swing, he saw. A number of men were lounging at the bar, a somewhat short but ornate affair; three or four couples were dancing to the muted music of a piano in the small corner reserved for such, and a few more were engaged in gambling, some bucking the chuck-a-luck cage, others trying their luck at poker and black-jack.

Glancing indifferently at the faces turned to him, Cameron located Ketty standing just within the dining section, a not large room off to one side, separated from the saloon and casino part of the building by a portiered archway. At once he crossed to where she waited, and returning her smile, sat down to one of the tables.

"Are you hungry?" she asked immediately.

Ketty was wearing a different dress, he saw—a tan-colored affair with a snowy-white shirtwaist over which was an apron, also white. She had pulled her hair to the top of her head to form a sort of dark crown, had shadowed her eyes, reddened her lips, and lightly powdered her cheeks—all of which made her a thoroughly beautiful woman, he decided.

"Not much—not after that fine meal you served. Reckon I could use some coffee and a piece of pie, however."

Ketty moved off toward a door in the rear that led to the kitchen, and Cameron glanced around. There were only two other tables occupied, each by a couple—one of which was being served by another waitress—Ketty's assistant, no doubt. The pie, fresh apple, and the coffee, strong and black the way he preferred it, arrived shortly with Ketty bringing a cup of the steaming liquid for herself. Placing the food before him, she sat down opposite, and studied him quietly as he began to eat.

"Was your place as bad as I've heard?"

He paused and a hardness filled his eyes. "It couldn't be much worse. They tore out the bridge that crossed the creek—sure was no need for that. House has been burnt to the ground, along with all the sheds and corrals."

Ketty shook her head sadly. "A shame. Where will you live if—"

"Bunkhouse is not too bad. Guess they've used it now and then as a line shack. Won't be hard to fix it up for the crew and me to live in."

Ketty said, "I see." Then, "John, I still don't understand what you intend to do. I know you plan to get back the stock Mason took over after you left, but you don't really figure to rebuild your ranch. I can't see why you—"

"Can put it all down as a way to force Mason's hand," he said, with a tight smile. "That's about the only way I can explain it."

He turned his attention then to the pie, finished it off, and took up the cup of coffee. "Been looking around in here—don't see anybody I know."

"Not much of a crowd tonight," Ketty replied. "Mostly people passing through. Most of the cowhands are from Muleshoe, although there's a couple there at the end of the bar I've never seen in here before. Tall man in the checked suit playing poker is a St. Louis drummer."

"Was sort of hoping to find some of the boys who worked for me hanging around, and seeing if they wanted their jobs back."

"Haven't seen any of them for over a year. I can't see what good three or four men will do if you intend to fight Mason. He's got a dozen or more—"

"Need just a couple or three to help me get my stock back, and then drive them to Silver City so's I can sell them. I'll have enough cash then to hire on a dozen guns of my own. Were you able to talk to any of the ranchers?"

"Passed the word along to the ones I saw—"

"How many?"

"Only three: Tom Lear, Claude Ivey, and Lige Davidson. None of the homesteaders have been in. Usually don't show up except on Saturdays."

"Was Davidson and the others interested?"

Ketty's shoulders stirred. "No, I'm afraid not."

Cameron swore softly, downed the last of his coffee. "Guess Sid and his crowd've still got them buffaloed," he said, pushing back his chair. "Reckon this is as good a time as any to start things to going."

Rising, he smiled reassuringly at the worried look crossing Ketty Griffin's smooth features and walked over to the bar. One of the men standing behind the counter, a portly individual in pants, shirt, collar, and vest, but no coat, moved up to him at once.

"What'll it be?"

"You Harry Kingman?"

"That's me, and I reckon you're the fellow I've been hearing about—John Cameron."

"Right. First off I want to say I'm obliged to you for sticking by the deal I had with Tom Briscoe."

"You're meaning Ketty. No need—was glad to. She's a mighty fine woman. What'll you drink?"

"Whiskey. Like for you to have one with me."

Kingman reached for a bottle and two glasses, set the latter on the bar in front of Cameron, and filled them. The men ranging along the counter had fallen silent, watching narrowly.

"Here's to prosperity!" the saloonkeeper said, and raised his glass.

Cameron smiled, matched the gesture, and downed his liquor. Laying a silver dollar on the counter, and pocketing the change when it came, he said, "I'm out to hire myself some help. Hope you won't mind me doing some asking around while I'm here."

Kingman brushed at his mouth to remove the drops of whiskey from his thick mustache. "No reason for me to say no, but I doubt you'll have much luck, judging from the talk I've heard."

"Sure is a lot of that going around," Cameron said indifferently. He took a step away from the bar. "Name's

Cameron," he called in a firm voice. "Got a ranch called the J-Bar-C north and west of here. Need two or three good men to do some cowboying and help me fix up the place."

"Hell, there ain't nothing left of that two-bit outfit but dust and ashes," a man along the counter observed.

"About right," Cameron agreed coolly, "but I ain't looking for opinions. I'm looking to hire on help."

There were a few moments of silence, and then a voice said in high disgust: "Any man would be a damn fool to go to work for you, Cameron! The minute the boss finds out you're stirring around up there he'll send down Bear and a couple other boys and plain clean you out."

Cameron folded his arms across his chest, and considered the rider thoughtfully. "Sounds like you're working for Sid Mason—Muleshoe."

"Just what I'm doing—along with a few more gents you see in here."

Cameron nodded. "Mind telling me your name?"

"Hell, no! I ain't ashamed of it. Folks call me Yocum—Danny Yocum."

"Well, Danny Yocum, you can tell Bear Kugan and Sid Mason that you saw me, and I told you I was starting up the J-Bar-C again, and if I catch any Muleshoe man on my range he'd best look out for his hide because I aim to shoot first and ask questions last."

Yocum was staring openmouthed at John Cameron, apparently unable to believe what he had heard. That any man would dare to challenge Sid Mason and mighty Muleshoe was beyond comprehension!

"Mister, you've either got a hankering to die, or else you're plumb loco!"

Cameron smiled tightly and turned his attention to the

saloon patrons in general. "Like I said, I can use two or three good cowhands if any of you are looking for work. I'm willing to pay the going rate, and while the sleeping won't be too comfortable until we can get things fixed up some, the eating will be good. And don't be scared of the Muleshoe outfit. I can take care of them."

"Like hell!" Yocum shouted. "I'll show you right now that—"

Cameron took three long strides forward. His balled fist lashed out—a cudgel of iron tempered by countless brawls inside the walls of the penitentiary—caught Danny Yocum on the side of the head. The man went down like a lightning-struck tree, his head rolling grotesquely on his shoulders.

Instantly three other Muleshoe riders surged forward, and for several moments John Cameron purged himself of the flaming anger that had piled up within him since he had first looked upon his ravaged ranch hours earlier, glorying in hammering at the faces—Muleshoe faces— that pressed in upon him from all sides, and driving them back to the floor.

And then suddenly in the swirl of confusion and wild yelling, more faces began to converge upon him, and the blows raining on his body increased. Other friends of Danny Yocum had decided to pitch in, do their part in bringing him down, Cameron realized. Jerking free, and backing away a few steps, he drew his pistol. Immediately the small crowd before him paused.

"Can take on two or three of you at a time," he gasped, wet with sweat and sucking hard for wind, "but if you aim to turn this into a gang fight, I expect I'd best even things up a bit."

There was some muttering among the Muleshoe men,

but after a bit they turned away and resumed their chairs at the tables or the places they'd occupied at the bar. Yocum had come back to his senses, and one hand pressed to his jaw, was being helped to his feet by two friends. As they started for the door, they halted. Yocum looked back.

"You better remember this ain't the last of this," he mumbled.

"Expect you're right," Cameron replied, his breathing again normal, and then as the trio continued on, he turned back to the remaining men.

"Anybody want to pick up where we left off?" he asked, his voice soft, almost inviting.

There was no response. "Make my offer again," he continued. "Any of you wanting a job ride out to my place before noon tomorrow. Can find it easy. Just follow the creek till you come to a burned-down house. I'll be there."

Nodding to Kingman, Cameron retraced his steps to the table where he had been sitting with Ketty Griffin. She was still there, worry showing in her eyes when she saw the bruises and smears of blood on his face. In the encounter the upper part of his shirt sleeves had burst under the stress of his straining muscles.

"You're hurt," she said, as he wiped at the blood. "And your shirt's ripped. I can—"

"No need to bother about any of it," he said, brushing aside her concern. "Been hurt worse shaving myself, and far as the shirt goes, it's old. These are the clothes I had when I went to the pen. They gave them back to me the day they turned me loose." There was a lightness in the tone of his voice, and his eyes were bright as he spoke.

Ketty studied him quietly for several moments, and then repeated her offer. "I can sew up those rips—"

"Obliged, but it'd be a waste of time. Aim to buy myself a whole new outfit when I get over to Silver City."

"No need to wear that rag till then. You could come on home with me so's I could doctor you up, fix the shirt—"

"Sure sounds mighty good, Ketty," he said, nodding, "but I'd best get back to my place. Can bet I'll be getting visitors before first light."

"Muleshoe?"

Cameron nodded, and laying a coin on the table to pay for the pie and coffee, got to his feet and turned away. "I'll be seeing you tomorrow, likely. Good night."

"Good night, John," Ketty replied. "And take care— for my sake."

CHAPTER 7

Cameron, having finished with the simple breakfast he'd prepared from his stock of grub, was sitting, his back to the sod wall of the bunkhouse, when the sound of an approaching horse brought him to his feet. Putting his cup of coffee aside, he hitched the pistol on his hip to a more convenient position, and now slouched against the corner of the squat structure, awaiting whoever was approaching.

He had been on the alert throughout the entire night, convinced that Sid Mason, once he heard of the encounter with Danny Yocum and the other Muleshoe cowhands in the High Ridge, and listened to what they'd been told to tell him, would send Kugan and some of his other men to square accounts and convince him it was wise to move on. But by sunup no one had appeared.

Cameron, knowing Mason well, was not deceived, Muleshoe's owner, bent on maintaining his position of power and mastery over the Red Rock Valley country, could not afford to let the incident pass—particularly where an old and dangerous enemy was concerned. Likely Yocum either failed to report the fight—feeling shame at being unable, even with help from several friends, to handle a single opponent—or he'd not had the opportunity as yet.

But Sid Mason, and Kugan, would know before the sun was much higher. If Yocum said nothing, there were the other Muleshoe riders present who would mention it, and so a fire would be lit. Cameron was glad of it; although he was far from ready, having hoped by that time to have a crew on hand, as well as several ranchers and home-steaders, to back his play, he was actually relieved that his plan to drive Sid Mason out of the country had been set in motion.

And this—not counting the shot one of Mason's men had taken at him when he first arrived in town—could be the opening move on the part of Muleshoe.

But it proved not to be. Shortly a fine-looking sorrel horse drawing a buggy came out of the trees and wheeled into the yard. Cameron's shoulders relaxed as tension drained from him. It was Darcy—Darcy Mason now, he reminded himself.

He let her pull up to the front of the bunkhouse, and then making no effort to hide his reluctance at seeing her, he moved away from the corner where he was standing and leisurely crossed to where she sat, prim and straight on the seat of the buggy. She watched him draw near, and when he halted, one hand resting on the vehicle's right front wheel, she spoke.

"How are you, John?"

Darcy had lost none of her beauty, Cameron saw, although there was a hint of dark circles under her eyes, and a weariness to her manner.

"Good enough," he said, taking note of the rifle lying on the floor of the buggy near her booted feet; for sport or protection, he wondered which.

Darcy frowned as she considered him. "Your face—it's cut and bruised, and your clothes are all torn. You've had some trouble."

"Nothing I wasn't able to handle."

"Was it some of Sid's men?"

He nodded. "What brings you here? I'm a bit out of the way if you're headed for town."

Darcy's shoulders stirred under the light dress she was wearing. One thing Cameron had always marveled at was her ability to continually appear fresh and crisp—as if she were on her way to church or some social affair.

"I—I wanted to see you," Darcy murmured after a bit of hesitation. "When I heard you were back I—"

"That shouldn't mean anything to you—you're a married woman now—Sid Mason's wife."

"I know," the woman replied in a falling voice, "but I wanted to see you anyway—again. Yesterday after I'd heard you were here I went to Ketty Griffin's house thinking I'd find you there. You had already gone."

"Came out here to see about fixing up my place. Take a look around. You can see what Sid and his bunch did to it."

Darcy did not move. "I know. He hates you more than anything or anybody else in this world—and now that you're back the trouble will start all over again."

"Just what I want," Cameron said coolly. "I'll never quit until I run him out of the valley—or one of us is dead."

Darcy shuddered at the violence in his voice and the

grim set of his battered features. "I'd hoped you'd never come back," she said finally, wearily.

"Can see that you never expected me to—you didn't lose any time marrying Sid."

The woman lowered her head, and folding her hands, stared at them. "Yes, I married him, but you have to understand, John—you'd been sent away for ten years, and most folks didn't think you'd ever live through all that time in the pen. I had to make myself believe that you were out of my life, forever."

Cameron listened still-faced, showing no reaction as his eyes reached out beyond her to the brushy hills running on indefinitely.

"I was tired—tired of working, tired of pushing off every drummer that came to town who seemed to think I was fair game because I was running Papa's restaurant— and I was sick of worrying over you, too, so when Sid started calling on me, and one day proposed marriage, I accepted. Was that so wrong? I had no hope of ever seeing you again."

"Seems you sort of expected me someday, else you wouldn't have taken my gun and money over to Ketty and told her to keep them for me."

Darcy shook her head helplessly. "I guess I was somehow hoping that you would come back. Anyway, I couldn't keep them at the house—Sid's house. He'd know that—"

The girl's voice broke, and her words ended. Cameron looked more closely at her. "He'd know what?"

She bit at her lower lip, and then resolutely faced him. "That I was still in love with you—no matter what!"

Cameron looked away. "Don't say that—it can't lead to anything."

"I know. You've always loved Ketty—I realized that

long ago—even when you thought you cared for me. And I'm married to Sid, no matter how I might feel personally. I made my choice, and good or bad, I'll stick by it . . . This trouble between you and Sid—I've heard what you've sworn to do. It can only end with a lot of men getting killed—even you and him."

"I don't figure on it being me," Cameron said bluntly.

Darcy shifted on the seat of the buggy, drew in the reins as the sorrel made a move to start. Face sober, she leaned toward Cameron.

"John, I once heard you say that vengeance was wrong. Have you changed your mind about it?"

"No—what I've got for Sid is pure hate. It's like when a man drives away or kills the wolf that's eating on his herd, it's hate that he feels, not vengeance."

Darcy was quiet for a long breath. Then, "I'm not sure of that. Maybe that's how you see it, and you keep telling yourself it's the truth, but I wonder—"

"Hate and vengeance aren't the same," Cameron cut in, shrugging. "A man can feel one without the other . . . Now, I expect you'd best be moving on. Everything's been said that needs saying—and I'm looking for a visit from your husband or some of his hardcases, or maybe both, any minute. Doubt if he'd take kindly to finding you here."

Darcy gave that brief thought, and gathered up the sorrel's lines. "No, I'm sure he wouldn't . . . Good-bye, John, I hope we'll see each other again."

"Best for you if we don't," Cameron said, and pivoting, started back to the bunkhouse.

CHAPTER 8

Scarcely had the grating sounds of Darcy Mason's iron-tired buggy wheels slicing into the sandy soil, and the thud of her horse's hoofs, died away when Cameron heard a step outside the bunkhouse doorway. In the act of adding more crushed beans to the coffeepot on the stove, and thinking it was either one of the ranchers or homesteaders he hoped to gather about him, or a cowhand coming in response to the job offer, he wheeled casually. Anger stiffened him as he recognized the grinning features of Bear Kugan.

"Howdy there, four-flusher," Kugan greeted, motioning with his pistol. "Get outside. The boss wants to do some talking at you—and you best put your hands up while I pull that iron you're packing."

Furious at himself for being so careless, Cameron moved to the door and stepped down onto the small landing, feeling Kugan lift his pistol from its holster, and hearing the thump of it as the Muleshoe man tossed it back into the sod house.

But that was secondary in his thoughts. At the edge of the yard a half-dozen riders were gathered in a half circle. In the center was Sid Mason. No lighter or heavier than Cameron remembered him, his thick blond hair pushed out from beneath his wide-brimmed, high-crowned hat, his small, sharp blue eyes as piercing as ever, and his mouth beneath a mustache, a hard, thin line as always. Astride a tall chestnut, and dressed in ordinary working ranch hand clothing, there was little to distinguish him from the men who rode for him other than his autocratic, ruthless bearing.

"You're a damned fool, Cameron!" he declared in a flat, straight-out way. "Should've never come back here."

Cameron, hanging tight to his temper, forced a humorless smile as he glanced at the men with Mason. Quint Redmon, brother of the man he'd gone to the pen for killing, dark and sullen; the Leavitt boys—Dan and Curly, both looking considerably older; and a lean, slouching rider with silver buttons in his hatband and a quiet, threatening way about him. This was the new man, Ben Lancaster, that Ketty had mentioned, he supposed: two more strangers—both youngsters that had to be three or four years shy of twenty—and of course Bear Kugan.

Kugan, still off his horse and standing close by, had grown heavier, stockier, and the width of his broad shoulders appeared to have increased. Dressed as always with shirt open down the front exposing the matted hair on his chest, he sported black cord pants, leather vest, wide-brimmed gray hat, and boots with fancy stitching. His beard and mustache, in contrast to his black eyes, were red.

"Here's where I belong," Cameron said finally, his voice cool. "And where I'll stay."

"It's where you'll get buried, I'm thinking," Kugan said.

Cameron shook his head. "Don't bet on it—leastwise not anytime soon."

Kugan laughed. "Pretty big talk! Hell, you damn near bought yourself a hole in the boneyard yesterday when you climbed out of that stage! Would've, too, if Quint there hadn't got the fidgets and missed."

Quint Redmon! So he was the bushwhacker who tried to gun him down. Fresh anger whipped through Cameron. As well settle with—

"Shut up, Bear!" Mason snapped, cutting in on Cameron's thoughts and turning his attention to him. "Want you to know that wasn't any of my doings—not that I would've minded him doing a good job of it. But Quint's still mighty fired up over his brother's killing. I've told him to forget it—"

Cameron shrugged. "Let me get my gun and he can have another try at settling up. Ain't no use in letting it drag on."

"No," Mason said, his voice flat and authoritative. "I don't want no shooting. Stanwyck knew I was coming by here. You and Quint can have it out some other time—if you're still alive."

John Cameron, thumbs hooked in the waistband of his pants, considered what Mason had said about Nate Stanwyck. Evidently Wolf Springs' new lawman was no hireling of the rancher after all—at least so far. The real test, Cameron suspected, was yet to come.

"Want to hear it straight from you, Cameron—what brought you back?"

Cameron folded his arms across his chest in the manner usual with him. "The job I started before you framed me and got me sent to the pen," he said firmly, "and that's to run you out of the country."

Kugan swore angrily, and the new man, Lancaster, shifted on his saddle to where he more squarely faced Cameron.

"Never mind, boys," Mason said, lifting a restraining hand, "I don't want no shooting." Shifting his attention then to Cameron, he wagged his head. "Still got that in your craw, I see. Best thing you can do is forget it—right now! I ain't the most patient man around. Anyway, you won't get nowhere with it."

"Could be things've changed. Folks maybe ain't like they were three or four years ago."

"Don't fool yourself—ain't nothing changed. If you think you're going to get them hayshakers and two-bit ranchers who sold out to me and then started bellyaching about me giving them a raw deal, if you expect them to back you, you're fooling yourself."

"Maybe," Cameron said calmly, eyeing Bear Kugan narrowly. Bear was spoiling for a fight—one which would come sooner or later, Cameron knew.

"And you ain't got no crew to side you," Mason continued. "Nobody around here's going to lift a hand for you—they got more sense than to buck me. Hell, man, use some sense!"

"I reckon I'll manage—"

Mason stirred impatiently, swiped at the sweat on his face with the back of a hand. "I ain't so sure of that. Now I'm going to warn you just one time, I—"

"Save your warning, Sid, and listen to mine. I aim to get back those two hundred steers of mine that you drove off my range, and then I—"

"Who says I took your steers?" Mason bristled.

"Never mind who—you've got them, and I'm taking them back."

"Just like that, eh? You want two hundred steers. Your just saying I've got them don't make it so. Seems to me you've got mighty little to go on."

"Enough. The U.S. marshal's office knows I had the steers, was trusting them to sell off the herd for me, but they never got around to it. Means the stock's still on my range, or ought to be—but it's not. And the only outfit around here who'd help themselves is Muleshoe."

"Damn it!" Kugan shouted. "You're calling us rustlers! I ain't going to stand for no talk like that."

"You claim you didn't rustle my herd? Letter I got from a friend while I was in the pen said the Leavitts and some other Muleshoe riders were seen pushing my stock onto Sid Mason's range. I expect you were close by while that was going on," Cameron said, level glance on Kugan.

Bear swore again, and drawing his pistol, took a step toward Cameron.

"Ain't nobody calling me a lousy rustler, specially a damned jailbird like you!"

Cameron rocked to one side, avoiding the blow that Kugan aimed at his head with the pistol. Cameron lashed out in that same moment with a knotted fist, rocking the squat redhead with a shocking right to the jaw. Kugan yelled, staggered, caught himself, and rushed in. Jamming his shoulder into Cameron, he knocked him off balance and down to one knee. And then before Cameron could recover, Kugan kicked him viciously in the ribs, sending him sprawling into the dust.

A yellow haze of anger swirled about John Cameron, minimizing the pain that surged through him, filling him only with the need to get at Bear Kugan. Rolling away from the redhead, he lunged to his feet, whirled. Kugan swung at his head, again with the pistol as a club. Cameron ducked, and drawing back his leg drove the toe of his boot into Bear's crotch.

"You want to fight that way—I expect I know how, too!" he rasped, and as Kugan buckled forward, he started an uppercut from his heels, and smashed it into Bear's jaw.

The blow seemed to lift the redhead off the ground, but it did not drop him. He shook his head as if to clear his muddled brain, cursed loudly, and charged. The pistol had dropped from his grasp, and now both fists were clenched and cocked as he closed in.

Cameron was waiting for him. As Kugan plunged in head on, Cameron jerked aside, brought a sledging blow downward that caught Bear on the temple, driving him flat onto the ground. Yells lifted from the rest of the Muleshoe crowd, words of encouragement, demands to Bear that he get up, finish the fight, and then through the hanging cloud of dust, above the shouting and his own labored breathing, Cameron heard Sid Mason's voice.

"Get in there and give Bear a hand, damn it! He's needing help!"

Immediately the Leavitts and Quint Redmon came off their horses and rushed in from three sides, all grinning wickedly. Lancaster and the two young riders made no move to participate, but settled back, as did Sid Mason, to enjoy the fun.

Cameron took a step backward, wheeled, caught Curly Leavitt unexpectedly, and staggered him with a quick left and right. He spun again but Redmon was waiting and drove a stiff blow to Cameron's jaw before he could throw up his guard. Almost in that same instant Dan Leavitt hammered half a dozen rock-hard fists into his middle.

Tightening his muscles as he'd learned to do, John Cameron fought back, but now Curly had recovered, and all three men began to punish him, driving blows to his head and body with the regularity of rain pounding a roof. Cameron struggled to stay upright, to maintain his flagging senses, but he knew he was wavering, and that he couldn't last much longer. Reaching out, he caught at the nearest shadowy figure and hung on. Vaguely, as if from a great distance, he again heard Sid Mason's voice.

"That's enough, boys. Don't want to kill him, leastwise not yet. This ain't the right time."

Immediately the hail of fists stopped. The man upon whom Cameron was leaning—Curly Leavitt—jerked free. Cameron, swaying uncertainly as his senses reeled, stared vacantly at the dim shapes moving away from him toward their horses.

"That there's a warning to move on." Sid Mason's voice again seemed to come from far off. "Telling you here and now, Cameron, I ain't going to put up with you. I catch you here again, I'll just let the boys do the job up good—once and for all . . . Let's go!"

In that next moment a hard blow to the jaw sent Cameron to his knees. Kugan! Bear was back on his feet, and making the most of his opportunity. Cameron threw up an arm to protect himself. It was to no avail. Brilliant lights flashed in Cameron's eyes as the redhead drove a fist again into his jaw and plunged him into a pit of darkness.

CHAPTER 9

John Cameron returned to reality feeling somewhat dazed—and wet. Puzzled, he sat up slowly, carefully, and glanced around. He was in the shade at the side of the bunkhouse. Eyes still a bit glazed, he settled them on the dim figures of three men in front of him, and endeavored to bring them into sharper focus. Two were hunched on their heels; a third was standing over him, hat in hand. It was dripping water.

"Friend," he heard a voice say, "you look like you been on the bottom of a stampede. Here, have yourself a shot of this red-eye. It'll put the fire back into you."

Cameron obediently accepted the bottle of liquor tendered him, and took a long swallow. The raw liquor hit his aching belly with shocking force, and almost at once, it seemed to him, his head began to clear.

"Obliged," he said, returning the bottle to the man who had offered it to him—a lean, scruffy-looking rider, probably in his forties, with a thin, sharp face and quick, dark eyes. He was dressed in ordinary cowhand clothing, but the pistol in the holster hanging loosely at his hip showed much use.

"I reckon you're welcome. Was you fighting that whole bunch of jaspers we met down the road a piece?"

Cameron stirred, pulling himself to a more erect sitting position. The man standing had dumped the remaining water from his hat and returned it to its place on his head.

"More or less. Name's John Cameron. Saying again I'm obliged to you."

"Ain't no need—just a mite sorry we didn't get here sooner so's we could've evened up the odds some. Always partial to a good ruckus—but I reckon you done pretty good on your own judging from the looks of a couple of them. I'm Ed Gorman," he continued, getting to his feet, as did the man squatting beside him. "Like for you to meet my pards. Fellow there with the wet hat's Virg Bratton. Other one's Turk Roper."

Cameron rose stiffly and shook hands all around. Bratton was a youngster, eighteen or so—a blond with a wildness about him as though he was on the lookout for trouble and excitement. Roper could be pegged as his opposite; older, somewhere in his thirties, he was short and thin, with the withdrawn manner of a man who lived by the gun he wore tied down to his leg.

As it was with Gorman they, too, wore the garb of cowhands—boots with heavy spurs, hard-finished pants of no particular color; plaid shirts, colorful neckerchiefs, and broad-brimmed hats. On the horses standing beyond them Cameron could see blanket rolls, slickers, and saddlebags bulging with extra clothing, personal articles, and likely a small supply of trail grub. Each also had a rifle slung in a boot, and a canteen.

Cameron considered it all without comment; such indicated clearly the three were men on the move, either eluding the law or simply drifting, searching for a place to settle down.

"Seen a lawman when he was coming through town," Roper said. "His name happen to be Henry?"

Cameron said, "No, it's Nate Stanwyck."

"That so? How long's he been around here?"

"Don't know exactly. Been away for a spell—three years in fact. Stanwyck took on the job while I was gone. He a friend of yours?"

Roper shrugged. "Ain't hardly," he replied, and looked off over the hills.

Cameron felt Ed Gorman's eyes studying him closely. "This here about you being gone for a spell—was you off in the pen somewhere?"

Cameron smiled wryly. "It show that plain?"

"Does, for a fact. Man learns how to look after hisself when he's cooped up in a place like the pen, and it sort of sticks out all over him. I savvy now how you was able to take on that whole bunch—or leastwise try to."

"Just what the hell was it all about?"

It was the younger man, Virg Bratton, who asked the question. Immediately Gorman wagged his head disapprovingly.

"It ain't fitting to go nosing into a man's private business—"

"Can't say that it's much private," Cameron cut in ruefully. "This is my ranch. Man by the name of Mason wants it—along with a dozen other places in the valley. I took it on myself to stop him."

Ed Gorman pursed his lips, nodded. "And I'm betting

it was him that got you sent to the pen when you started tromping on his toes."

"You're right—framed me for murder. Was turned loose after serving three years of a ten-year stretch."

"He that sort of yellow-haired fellow we seen riding a big chestnut with white stockings?" Roper wanted to know.

"That was him. Sid Mason. Owns the Muleshoe ranch. Covers about everything in this part of the country now—says he wants a million acres."

"And you've come back from the pen, aiming to start bucking him all over again, that it?" Gorman said, frowning. "You sure you ain't holding a busted flush?"

"Could be," Cameron admitted, "but that's neither here nor there. I'm going to run him and his crowd out no matter what it takes. Was hoping I could round up some of the homesteaders and ranchers that Mason crooked, or is about to take over, to back me, but so far nobody's showed up."

"You for sure ain't meaning to go after that jasper by yourself, are you?"

"Nope, not if I can help it. Don't think I'd get very far, big as Muleshoe is—but I'll sure give it a try if it comes down to that. Planning on riding over to Silver City, town west of here, and hiring myself a crew—"

"Punching cows or fighting?" Virg Bratton asked quickly.

"Little of both. Mason's bunch drove two hundred steers of mine off my range while I was gone. Have to get them back so's I can raise the cash to do what I'm figuring on."

"What's wrong with hiring some of them saddle-warmers we seen standing around your town—Wolf Springs?"

"Tried last night, but Mason's got everybody scared to

even talk to me much less hire out. Even had trouble
buyin' grub from an old friend of mine that runs the
store."

"I reckon we can fix that," Roper said. "Just you
pencil out a list of what you're wanting, and me and the
kid'll go get it for you."

"Obliged to you, but no. Man that owns the place, like
I said, was a friend of mine once—would be again if it
wasn't for Mason. Don't want to make things hard for
him."

"Then where'll you get your grub?"

"Same place I figure to get a crew—Silver City. Ain't
far from here—half a day or so," Cameron explained,
tenderly exploring the side of his face, now dark with
numerous swellings.

A silence followed Cameron's words during which all
four men turned their attention toward the cottonwood
trees where a commotion of some sort between several
scrub jays was breaking the heated quiet. Then Gorman,
glancing at Roper and Virg Bratton, pulled off his hat
and scratched at the back of his head.

"You real particular about this here crew you're aiming
to hire?"

"Nope, just looking for men who'll help me get my
stock back, lend me a hand around here—and won't be
afraid to use their gun when the time comes—which it
sure'n hell will."

Gorman touched his friends again with a side glance,
reset his hat. "You reckon we could fill the bill? We're
heading south for the Mexican border, but we ain't in no
powerful big hurry."

"No, sir, we sure ain't!" Bratton added hurriedly. "And

this here little ruckus you're planning sure does sound mighty interesting."

Cameron considered the three men with a growing smile. They were made to order for what he wanted and needed—if they could be controlled; and that could be a chore where Turk Roper and Virg Bratton were concerned.

"Doubt if I could find anybody better than you three," Cameron said, "but I best make a couple of things clear. I don't want killing just for the sake of killing. And my quarrel's with Sid Mason and some of the bunch he had with him today—rest of the Muleshoe people are just working there. And Roper," he added, turning his attention to the quiet gunman, "if you've got something against Marshal Stanwyck I want you to forget it while you're working for me."

Roper's jaw hardened briefly, and then looking away, he spat. "Something me and him'll settle one of these days—now that I've caught up with him."

"Your business—I don't want no lawman's blood on my hands. Same goes for my friends in town. Stay clear—"

"They sure ain't what I'd call friends if they're like the store fellow," Roper mumbled.

"Me neither," Virg Bratton added, "but you're the he coon around here far as I'm concerned, and what you say goes with me. We all riding to this here Silver City to load up on grub?"

Cameron had thought that far, but he shook his head at once. "No, I'd like for you all to stay here and look after the place. Good chance Mason or some of his bunch will come back to finish tearing down what's left of it. If there's somebody here—"

"You want us to just set back and not hurt nobody if they do?" Roper asked acidly.

"Do whatever you have to— just don't let them do any more damage. Won't be any of my friends among them."

Roper nodded his satisfaction. Ed Gorman scrubbed thoughtfully at his chin. "Means you'll be making the ride to this here town by yourself. I don't figure that's very smart, not the way that bunch feels about you. Would suit them real good to catch you out somewheres by yourself—and you can bet they're keeping an eye on you. I reckon I'd better track right along with you. Turk and Virg can look after the place. Anyway, you'll be needing extra horses to pack in the supplies you're bringing back."

"Was planning to borrow one of your mounts for a pack animal—"

"Can take Virg's—he's carried pack before. And with what we can hang on yours and mine, should be enough. When we lighting out?"

"Right away. Leave the saddle on Virg's horse, I don't have a regular pack rig. Can sack the supplies and tie them on easier."

Cameron was already moving toward his horse. Ed Gorman followed his lead, and shortly both men were mounted, with Gorman trailing Bratton's horse behind him at the end of a short rope.

"Any ranchers or homesteaders show up wanting to talk to me," Cameron said, pausing to speak to Roper and Virg, "tell them to come see me tomorrow."

"Sure, long as they're friendly," Roper said dryly. "When do you figure to be back?"

"Silver City's a good half day's ride by trail. Can look for us around midnight."

"Midnight," Roper repeated. "Well, you best sing out

when you get close. Hate to shoot one of you in the dark, thinking you was some of them Muleshoe boys . . . Now, don't forget to bring me back some liquor. I'm getting low."

Cameron smiled, and nodded. "We'll remember," he said, and rode on out of the yard with Gorman at his side. He would take time to go by Ketty's, tell her of his good fortune in finding a crew, and that he was on his way to Silver City for supplies, in the event something with the ranchers and homesteaders developed and she came looking for him.

There had been little talk between them as they rode on through the heat to the settlement of Silver City. However, after all business was transacted, which included, besides the necessary stock of groceries and other needed items, a new shirt for Cameron and conversation with a local cattle buyer relative to the sale of his herd, followed by a good meal and a couple of drinks at the Malpais Saloon where they also obtained two quarts of liquor for Turk Roper, and they were headed homeward, both men opened up considerably.

Gorman and his two friends, while being on the way to Mexico, were not running from the law, Cameron learned. Turk was a gunman who hired out on occasion to do a job, but had always managed to keep his nose clean. Lawmen had no claim against him—they just didn't want him around.

"Seem to think he draws trouble," Gorman explained, "and maybe he does—but I sure ain't never seen nothing he couldn't handle—badge-toter or otherwise."

"How about Bratton? Got kind of a wild look in his eyes."

"Oh, the kid's all right. Kind of wild, sure, but you got to expect that. Was the same at his age. He's hell for having himself a big time—fighting or funning with women. But he's a good one to ride the river with."

Cameron had nodded to signify his understanding as they rode steadily on. Both his horse and Ed Gorman's had full saddlebags and several flour sacks that bulged with groceries slung over the back of their hulls. Bratton's animal was well draped with half a dozen more sacks attached to its saddle as well as carrying packed leather pouches. It had cost Cameron a good part of his capital, it being necessary to pay cash for everything he'd bought, but he was not too concerned about that now; he had a crew, and getting back his rustled herd, which would be sold off immediately, would not be any big job.

"Reckon, you're wondering about me—"

At Gorman's statement Cameron shifted, shook his head. "Up to you, Ed. I'm no hand to dig into a man unless he leads off first."

"Well, hiring out to you I figure you've got a right to know. I ain't nothing more'n a working cowhand, least-wise up to a couple of years ago. A bit before that I was in the pen for killing a man. Run into Turk when I got out, and we sort of teamed up. Been sort of drifting around together ever since—working when we was in need of eating or drinking money, taking it real easy the rest of the time. Virg threw in with us about six months ago. Looks at things same way me and Turk does—work when we have to, just plain enjoy living when we don't."

"Not for sure how long this job with me will last," Cameron said. "Maybe a few days—maybe a month."

Gorman grinned disarmingly. "Ain't likely we'd be interested in working permanent-like."

"That's good—and I want you and the others to know that I appreciate your lining up with me. Doing what I have to do alone was shaping up to be quite a chore."

Gorman drew one of the quarts of liquor from his saddlebags, hung the reins of the horse he was riding on the horn, and pulled the bottle's cork. Offering it first to John Cameron, who had a generous swallow, he then treated himself. That done, Gorman corked and returned the container to its place, smacked his lips, and wiped his mouth.

"Been puzzling over that," he said. "Just what are you fixing to do? From what you told us this morning I got the idea you was a mite touched in the head—if you don't mind me saying so. You're taking on a big job, and it seems like you've got a plenty of folks against your doing it."

Cameron smiled, stirred about on his saddle. "Been told before I was loco, so it don't bother me none," he said, and set forth the details of the job he'd undertaken— to rid the Red Rock Valley country of Sid Mason— beginning with the time when he had his small ranch under way, and did part-time deputy marshal work to help make ends meet, and then, because of his opposition to Sid Mason, the incident that led up to his being sent to prison for murder, and his recent return.

"The rest you mostly know about—coming by right

after Mason and his bunch worked me over, and telling me to move on, or else."

Gorman scrubbed at his jaw. "Sticking your neck out mighty far for some folks who don't seem to give a damn, seems to me."

"They're scared. Figure if they show they're friendly and willing to side me—even if they're about to lose their place—they're scared of what Mason and his bunch will do to them."

"And you're willing to go right ahead, anyway—"

"Made up my mind to that when I was in the pen sweating it out," Cameron said. "Decided that a man like Sid Mason had no right to throw his weight around, tromp on decent, hard-working people, and get his way just because he had money and a gang of hardcases to fetch and carry for him. Swore to myself that when I got out—and he was still alive and running roughshod over folks in the valley—I'd pick up where I left off, and start in after him. Maybe it does sound like I'm a looney, but it makes sense to me, and it's something I've got to do."

Gorman leaned back in his saddle, and pulling off his hat, swiped at the sweat on his forehead. The lowering sun, now almost to the western horizon, was at their backs, and while the heat still held, traveling was not so bad.

"Reckon I can understand that," he said. "Been a few things I felt I just plain had to do—like killing that sonofabitch I went to the pen for. Knew that's where I'd wind up when I started out to do it, but I had to go right ahead, anyway. Just how do you—"

Cameron had drawn himself to attention. His eyes—

narrowed to cut down the haze spreading across the land—were fixed on the trail where it cut down into a wash a short distance farther on.

"Something bothering you?" Gorman continued, noting the frown on Cameron's face.

"On down a ways—saw riders. Three or four of them. They split up. Could be waiting for us."

"Ambush—that what you're thinking?" Gorman said, craning his neck to see.

"That's my guess. Of course, it could be just a bunch of cowhands on the way to Silver City."

"We'd be smart to figure it ain't," Gorman observed dryly. "You figure they've seen us?"

"Probably saw us back a piece when we were more in the open. With all this brush and rocks they likely haven't spotted us along here."

"You want to dodge them?"

Cameron gave that thought. The riders could be cowhands, but most likely they were some of Mason's men, having learned somehow of the trip he and Gorman were making to Silver City, and taking advantage of a fine opportunity to kill him.

"No. I'd as soon they find out now that they're not driving me off."

Ed Gorman bobbed approvingly. "Just what I was expecting you to say. Now, how do you want to do this?"

"I'll keep going on the trail, you cut away, and circle around. When they stop me you be setting there in the brush with that rifle you've got in your hands—all ready to join the party."

Gorman chuckled happily. "Sounds right interesting!

Turk and Virg are sure going to be disappointed when I tell them what they missed."

If they have missed anything, Cameron thought as he and Gorman rode on. It was entirely possible that Sid Mason, being aware of his absence, had sent some of his crew to pay the ranch a destructive visit.

CHAPTER 10

~~~~~~

He was taking a long risk, Cameron realized, as he rode slowly on. If the riders he'd seen turning into the brush were Muleshoe men—and he was almost certain they were—they would have orders from Sid Mason to shoot and quickly bury the results.

The trail began to drop steeply into a wide, brush-filled arroyo. Overhead the sky was clear. The sun, an hour or two yet before setting, continued to bear down without respite, and twice Cameron pulled out his ban-danna and mopped at the sweat lying on his face and misting his eyes. His clothing seemed plastered to his taut body, but he thought little of that; his mind was concentrating on the thick growth now only a dozen strides ahead into which he had seen the riders disappear.

He had seen no further signs of Ed Gorman. The man, leading Virg Bratton's heavily loaded horse, would be off to his left, and such would put him slightly above the wash through which he was riding. A hard grin split Cameron's dry lips; if Gorman misjudged, overshot, and came into the arroyo below where the riders were waiting, and thereby was forced to double back—he just could be late getting to the party!

That would come as no big surprise, Cameron thought grimly as he slid the holstered forty-five on his hip to a more forward, convenient position. Just about anything he ever undertook, it seemed he had to go it alone. He reckoned it was better that way—always being on his own. Never having to depend on anyone simplified a lot of problems.

The brush was immediately ahead. The buckskin Cameron was riding pricked his ears and looked nervously about, the whites of his eyes betraying his fear. There were men in the tangled brush, that was for certain—just as it most certainly was an ambush.

Cameron jerked the gelding to a halt. Bear Kugan and Quint Redmon had appeared suddenly on his right. To his left the Leavitt brothers took up a stand in the center of the trail. All were holding drawn guns.

"We been waiting for you," Bear said with a wide grin.

"Yeh, and you sure ain't no pretty sight," Curly Leavitt commented, laughing. "Now, where you reckon he got all them cuts and bruises? You reckon he's been in a ruckus somewhere?"

"Sure was," Kugan replied, "but he sure didn't learn nothing from it."

Anger simmering within him, and aware that Ed Gorman was still somewhere off in the brakes, Cameron settled back in his saddle and let his arms settle slowly to his sides.

"What do you want, Bear?" he demanded, knowing full well the answer, but hoping to gain time.

"Why, you, Mister Cameron!" Kugan said. "You think

we rode all this way out here just to pick daisies? When Sid seen that you wasn't taking his advice to ride on, he give us the word to take care of you—"

"You won't shoot me, Bear. Too many people know I'm around—the marshal for one."

"Stanwyck? Hell, Sid's done fixed things up with him. He ain't no worry. And far as other folks, why we'll just throw you in that wash over there, kick dirt down on you, and nobody'll ever know what happened."

"Probably figure he saddled up and rode on just like the boss told him to do," Quint Redmon said.

"Ain't likely," Cameron countered. "Folks know me better than that."

Redmon swore, brushing at the sweat trapped in his whisker stubble. "What the hell are we wasting time palavering with this jailbird for? Boss said to get rid of him and not fool around doing it." Quint paused, eyeing Bear Kugan suspiciously. "You ain't getting cold feet, are you?"

Kugan swore loudly. "You ever see me get cold feet about doing anything?"

"No, can't say as I have, but—"

"Well, there's just a couple of things that we best decide about first—that buckskin he's riding for one. Got to figure what to do with him because he's the kind of a horse a man don't forget. And all the sacks he's toting. Would've bought the stuff he's got in them at the general store in Silver City. Means they'll recollect him being there if anybody comes along asking questions."

"You reckon he's just stocking up so's he can pull out?" Curly Leavitt wondered.

"No, he ain't pulling out—he's done made that plain,"

Redmon said. "I ain't about to let him if he was. Still owe him for my brother."

"Brand got what he asked for," Cameron stated coldly, glancing again to his left for some indication of Ed Gorman. "Drew on me. I had no choice but to shoot."

"That's a damned lie, and you know it!" Quint shouted. "My brother didn't have no gun on him!"

"He had one, all right," Cameron said quietly. "Somebody helped it disappear after the shooting. Use your head—you ever know Brand to go anywhere without his gun?"

Quint frowned, shook his head. "Your talking ain't doing no good. I know what I seen."

"Maybe you did, but did it ever occur to you that maybe Bear, or one of the other Muleshoe bunch that was hanging around, picked up Brand's gun and hid it before the marshal got there so's it would look like murder? Mason was wanting to get rid of me real bad at that time, and when Brand didn't plug me right off, and I got him instead, it opened the door for Sid to frame me—get me out of the way. You ever stop to think that was how it could've happened?"

"Now who's wasting time yammering?" Kugan asked in a loud voice as Redmon started to make a reply. "Quint, if you're in such a all-fired hurry to get this done and square up for Brand, why don't you get at it?"

"Just what I'll do!" Redmon replied, and leveling his pistol, cocked it.

The hot stillness burst with the crack of a gunshot coming from the brush off to Cameron's left. The horses all jumped, startled by the unexpected blast, and shied wildly. Quint Redmon gasped, threw up his arms, and slowly fell from the saddle.

"Anybody else got a notion like him?"

Ed Gorman's drawling voice broke the hush that followed the rolling echoes of the rifle. Cameron, his own weapon out and in hand now, faced Kugan and the two Leavitts with a twisted smile. He should have known Gorman would be there—probably was all the while—just waiting to make a move, if needed.

"Put your iron away, Bear," Cameron said, motioning with the barrel of his gun. "Goes for you Leavitts, too—if you're wanting to stay alive."

Kugan's mouth was a tight line, and fury brightened his eyes. He was no doubt wondering how he would explain the turnabout that took the play away from him—and cost the life of Quint Redmon—to Sid Mason.

Again Gorman's rifle split the late afternoon's stillness. Dust spurted over the hoofs of Bear Kugan's horse, starting the animal dancing away. Immediately the three Muleshoe men holstered their weapons.

"Who the hell is that?" Kugan wanted to know, staring in the direction from which the shots had come.

Cameron, having a bit of difficulty with his own buckskin, who didn't like the sound of the gunshots, smiled. "Friend of mine. You can tell Sid that not every man around is scared of him, and—"

"I'll tell you something," Bear cut in, "shooting Quint's going to let down all the bars because Sid ain't going to let it pass—"

"Well, you can tell him my name's Ed Gorman," the man said, riding out of the brush and lining up beside Cameron. The pack horse he had been leading evidently had been tethered somewhere back along the course he had followed. "Now, if he'd like to take this up personal-like with me, I'll be mighty happy to accommodate him.

Goes for you or anybody else working for him, too. You can find me at Cameron's place."

"You working for him?" Kugan asked.

"Yes, sir—seven days a week. Nights, too."

Bear spat, then glanced off to the south where a dozen or so vultures were circling slowly in the darkening sky.

"You made a big mistake taking a job with Cameron," he said. "Bigger one when you plugged Quint."

"I reckon the mistake was you jaspers fixing to bushwhack us. I'm wishing now that all of you had thrown down on Cameron. Could've given your friend lying there some company when he reached hell. Fact is, it's still a right good idea!"

Gorman's narrow features were quiet, and his eyes appeared soft and friendly, betraying none of the violence that lay beneath the surface. It was clear to John Cameron the man would do as he was suggesting with the slightest provocation, and be smiling all the while. Turk Roper was the member of the trio that he'd pegged as a killer; it looked now as if Gorman deserved equal status.

"I'm obliged to you, Ed, for stepping in when you did," Cameron said, his tone level, conciliatory, "but there's no need for more. One dead man's enough."

Gorman's casual manner did not alter. He continued to study Bear Kugan and the Leavitts in his amiable sort of way, all the while keeping his rifle leveled at them.

"I reckon you're the boss, Mister Cameron," Gorman said, "but a fellow sure ought to kill every snake that cuts his trail because there ain't no telling when it's liable to crawl up on him out of the brush."

Cameron nodded, agreeing. He was still not certain of Ed Gorman, and was endeavoring to handle the tall, half-smiling man with care. One dead man was enough for that day, and it would serve the purpose, for Sid Mason was now in the position of having to make a move—and thus the war would begin.

"Load up, Kugan, and get him back to Mason's place," Cameron directed, motioning to Bear. "You're not leaving him here for the buzzards."

Kugan gestured at the Leavitt brothers, who climbed off their saddles, caught up Redmon's horse, and hung the rider's body across the saddle. Tying it down, they remounted.

"Now, move out," Cameron ordered. "Stay on the trail—and don't get any fancy notions. We'll be right behind you."

"Going to be dark soon," Curly Leavitt muttered as they turned to ride on. "Maybe you won't be seeing us."

"Don't bank on it," Cameron replied. "Could be you won't know just where we are, but we'll be there keeping an eye on you—Gorman with his rifle, and me with my forty-five. My advice to you is ride straight back to Muleshoe."

It had been late in the evening when Cameron and Ed Gorman, announcing their approach with shouts, arrived at the ranch. They had experienced no further trouble from Bear Kugan and the Leavitts, all apparently taking Cameron's warning seriously and making no effort to strike back. Both Cameron and Gorman were weary from the long ride, and lost no time in finding their bunks after making a quick meal from the supplies they had brought in.

Earlier, as they were drinking their coffee Roper had asked, "Reckon we ought to keep watch? We didn't have no visitors here today, but after hearing about the trouble you had on the trail, it just could be some of them Muleshoe boys'll be dropping by."

"It would be a good idea," Cameron agreed. "We can break down the night into four—"

"Ain't no need for that," Roper said, uncorking one of the bottles of whiskey brought him from Silver City. "I ain't much for sleeping—specially when I got a friend to keep me company." He patted the bottle of liquor fondly. "You fellows are powerful tired—and so's the kid. I'll just set out there in the brush and keep my eyes peeled, and do the watching. Maybe I can have me a little fun, like you two birds did."

At that Turk Roper had taken up a rifle and bottle, and hanging a blanket about his narrow shoulders, walked off into the moonlit night.

Cameron had glanced questioningly at Gorman, at the moment rising and moving toward the bunkhouse where Virg Bratton was already snoring peacefully.

"Hadn't we best spell him off after a bit? Don't seem right him having to stand guard all night."

"Don't fret about old Turk," Gorman said. "He knows what he's doing—and like he said, sleeping ain't never been important to him."

Thus it was arranged. There was no need for the precaution, however. When daybreak came with the first salmon streaks reaching up into the sky there had been no signs of Muleshoe riders, and things were quiet around the sod bunkhouse as Cameron set about putting together a breakfast. It was to be a one-time treat as he had brought back a couple of dozen eggs which he fried with bacon and sliced potatoes. Fresh bread, also obtained in Silver City, warmed in the oven of the stove, and strong, black coffee completed the meal.

When it was over Virg Bratton wiped his mouth with the back of a hand, smacked appreciatively, and declared, "If this is the kind of grub we'll be getting around here, I'm for staying on right up to dying time!"

Gorman seconded the comment, and Turk Roper nodded in his usual, noncommittal way. He was disappointed that no raid by Muleshoe was attempted during the night, and let it be known that he felt cheated. As for Cameron, while he was certain Sid Mason would not let matters ride for long, he was grateful there had been no trouble during the night; he hoped to have the bunkhouse and the surrounding area better prepared when it did come.

"What d'you want us to do today?" Gorman asked. "Go after them cows that was took from you?"

"Not yet. Think we'd better get a corral built for the horses first. Can cut a few saplings, and drag in some brush, build it between the bunkhouse and that first cottonwood."

Bratton sighed. "I sure ain't never found no shovel that fit my hands—"

"I reckon you will today," Gorman said. "Or maybe you'd rather take the ax and cut them saplings we'll be needing."

"Ain't seen no ax handle that fit either," Virg grumbled, "but I expect I can manage. Just point me towards them trees, and I'll get busy."

Cameron nodded to Ed Gorman. "I'll leave it up to you while I finish fixing up inside the bunkhouse so's it'll be livable. Soon as I'm done, I'll come out and give you a hand."

Gorman started for the door, shifted his eyes to Roper, lounging against its frame. "How do you feel about working, Turk?"

Roper drew himself up straight, shrugged. "I'll do my share," he said, and followed Bratton into the yard.

Gorman grinned at Cameron, and said in a low voice. "Turk just ain't partial to work of no kind. Shows how much he thinks of you when he'll cotton to using an ax or a shovel . . . See you later."

Gorman left the bunkhouse, and Cameron turned to straightening and rearranging its interior in hopes of making it more suitable as well as comfortable for the use of four men. He had done about all possible along such lines when the faint thump of a horse approaching at a lope reached him. Dropping a hand on the pistol on his hip, making certain it was in place, and feeling tension rise within him, he crossed to the doorway. He still didn't feel ready for a confrontation with Sid Mason and his crowd, but reckoned it might as well come then as later. But it was not Muleshoe; instead it was Town Marshal Nate Stanwyck.

The lawman, hat pulled low on his head, mustache bristling, rode up to the bunkhouse and halted opposite the doorway. Crossing his arms over his chest, Cameron stepped out onto the short landing. Off to his left Gorman had paused at the business of digging post holes for the corral; there was no sign of either Bratton or Turk Roper, both of whom were evidently off cutting saplings and gathering brush.

"Expect you know why I'm here," Stanwyck began in a harsh voice. He had waited for the customary invitation to step down, but all things considered Cameron had not extended it; thus the lawman remained mounted.

"Maybe I do—"

Off to the north the faint sound of a dog barking could be heard in the comparative hush, and down along Texhama

Creek, a migrant mallard duck quacked noisily. The morning air was already warm, and the day bid fair to be a hot one.

"A killing—that's why!" Stanwyck snapped. "Quint Redmon. Man working for you shot him down. I'm here to take him in whoever he is."

"Mason send you? Heard yesterday that he was telling you what to do nowadays."

Stanwyck flushed angrily, stirred on his saddle. "That's a damn lie. I ain't—"

"Makes no difference to me," Cameron cut in with a shake of his head. "You're against me no matter what. But you best get this shooting straight. Quint threw down on me, would've blown me off my horse if a man working for me hadn't shot him first."

Stanwyck, frowning deeply, said, "Not the way it was told to me."

"If the story's any other way, it's wrong. It was an ambush. Quint, Bear Kugan, and the Leavitts were all in on it. We spotted them in time and—"

"Howdy, Deke—"

At Turk Roper's words, coming from the corner of the bunkhouse, Stanwyck came sharply about. His eyes flared, and he drew himself up straight in the saddle.

"Turk—it's you!" he said in a tight voice.

Roper, hands hanging slackly at his sides, moved farther into the open. Beyond him Virg Bratton appeared, took up a stand also near the sod structure, while Ed Gorman, having forsaken his work near the cottonwoods, was closing in slowly from that side of the yard.

Stanwyck recovered himself somewhat. "He—Turk working for you, too?" he asked, nodding at Roper.

"Sure is. Got myself a fine crew—something you and others around here didn't think I could do."

Stanwyck, eyes never leaving Roper, swore deeply. "Means there'll be hell around here for sure now. I heard Aaron Wilson called you a firebrand. He was right. This valley ain't going to see nothing but blood from now on considering the kind of help you've hired."

Cameron smiled. "If you ain't working for Sid Mason, you can stop it before it starts."

"Stop it—how the hell can I do that?"

"Get Sid to return the land he crooked all those folks out of, and leave the country."

Stanwyck pulled off his hat and shook his head. In the bright sunlight his white hair seemed to throw back the light as he moved.

"Hell—you know I can't do that—"

Cameron, keeping a close watch on Turk Roper for any sign of trouble, said, "Why? Because you know he'd not listen, or because you're working for him, and are scared to talk up?"

"I'm saying again I ain't beholden to Mason, and far as being scared—" Stanwyck began, restoring his hat.

"You always was long on guts when you was holding the whip handle and had plenty of friends standing around to back you," Roper cut in coldly. He was a motionless shape in the driving sunlight, giving the appearance of being coiled and ready to strike at any instant. "You're mighty good at hoorawing folks, too."

Stanwyck seemed to withdraw into himself. "That was a long time ago, Turk, and best forgot."

"No—time don't make no difference to me—"

"It ought. Reckon you've done some fool stunts in your life that you'd as soon forget."

"Maybe—but I ain't you, and you ain't me, and that's where the trouble's coming from. I—"

"You can tell Sid Mason to forget trying to hang another murder charge on me, or any man working for me," Cameron cut in hastily, seeing all the signs now of erupting violence in the offing. "Best thing you can do, Marshal, is get off my land, and stay off. Far as I'm concerned you're just another Muleshoe hired hand."

Stanwyck's color deepened. He seemed about to make a retort, changed his mind, and wheeling his horse about, struck for town at a good lope.

For a long minute there was silence, and then Gorman drawled, "Now, there ain't no cause for you to go wet nursing me—I ain't no dogie calf that needs looking after. If that tin star thinks he's big enough to haul me in and jug me, I'd be real pleased to see him try."

"Just returning a favor—one that was worth my life," Cameron said in a placating voice.

"Same goes for me," Roper said. "Been seeing to my hide for quite a spell. Reckon I can keep right on."

Cameron put his attention on the gunman. "Nobody's doubting that, but I've already told you settle your beef with Nate Stanwyck some other time. I don't care much one way or another about what happens to him; I just don't want you killing him on my land. That'd make things a lot worse."

"Killing's a killing no matter whose land it's on," Virg Bratton remarked sagely.

"Not denying that," Cameron agreed, "but I need to keep my nose clean for as long as I can . . . Let's get back to work."

They resumed their various labors, broke for a bit of dinner at noon, and then, Cameron having completed the necessary work inside the bunkhouse he joined the other men in building the corral and trenching water to its lower end for the convenience of the horses.

Around the middle of the afternoon, just as they were finishing up the job, Bratton paused and glanced toward the north.

"Somebody coming," he announced. "Sounds like a horse and buggy—or maybe it's a buckboard." A moment later he added: "Buggy—and a woman's driving it."

Cameron muttered a curse, and turned toward the road. It would be either Ketty Griffin or Darcy, and with the situation at an explosive stage, he wanted neither around.

"Now, that there's what I call a pretty woman," Virg continued as the buggy drew closer. "Fact is she's just about the prettiest gal I've set my eyes on since Dodge—"

"Happens she's Sid Mason's wife," Cameron broke in, and walked out into the yard to meet the woman, wondering as he did what would bring her there. It had to be something serious, he judged, else Darcy would not have risked coming.

"What's the matter?" he greeted, stepping in close to a front wheel as she drew to a stop.

Darcy's features were strained, and her dark eyes were filled with concern. She appeared agitated, and in a great hurry.

"Bear—Bear Kugan and about a dozen men," she said in a rush of words, "they're coming here after you and the man who killed Quint Redmon. I heard Sid tell them to settle with you and him—and not to come back if they didn't."

Darcy paused, looked back over a slim shoulder. "They can't be far behind me, John—you've just got time to mount up—go."

Cameron shook his head. "I won't be going anywhere. Truth is, this is what I've been waiting for, and—"

"Lady is sure right," Virg Bratton called. "Can hear riders coming up fast!"

Cameron did not hesitate. "You men take cover," he ordered, and hurriedly climbed into the buggy beside Darcy. Gathering up the lines, he added, "I'll get the lady out of sight behind the bunkhouse, and head her into the brush so nobody'll know she was here—then I'll be back."

CHAPTER 11

It took only moments to drive Darcy in behind the low bunkhouse. Leaping to the ground, Cameron pointed to the trees and brush some thirty yards or so distant.

"Head for there!" he shouted, slapping the horse sharply on the rump.

As the sorrel plunged away, Cameron spun and started back for the yard. He could hear the pound of horses rushing onto the hardpack fronting the sod house and realized they had swept in much sooner than anticipated; but they would not see Darcy as she raced for cover; the intervening bunkhouse would block their view of her.

Gunshot erupted in the yard, and yanking out his pistol, Cameron ran to take his place with Gorman and the others. A riderless horse suddenly appeared at the corner of the bunkhouse, and close behind it Kugan with two riders Cameron did not recognize spurted into sight.

"There he is!" Bear shouted in surprise, and veering his horse sharp right, rode directly at Cameron. The pair with him instantly followed suit.

Cameron snapped a shot at Kugan, and threw himself to one side. His bullet missed, as did those Kugan and the other Muleshoe men leveled at him. But escape was not possible. All three riders bore in on him at full speed, forcing their unwilling horses to slam into him, knock him aside, and down.

"Hold up!" he heard Kugan shout in a hard voice. "Got a little score to settle with this bastard before I put a bullet in his head!"

Dazed, Cameron attempted to roll away, get back on his feet, but Kugan was on him before he could rise. Pain shocked Cameron as Bear drove a booted foot into his groin, sending him staggering to one side, and down once more.

"Boss said we wasn't to do no fooling around with this jasper—that we was to fix him permanent," one of the other Muleshoe men said in a protesting voice. "I ain't—"

"I know what he said!" Kugan shouted through the lifting dust. "Get down here and hold the sonofabitch while I get in a few good licks! Then you can drag him off into the brush and fill him plumb full of holes!"

The words seeped dimly into John Cameron's pain-filled brain as he struggled to regain his feet, while the sound of guns out in front of the bunkhouse was a vague staccato. Sucking for breath, he managed to draw himself upright, realizing as he did that he'd dropped his gun when the horses shouldered into him. Numbly he began to glance about, searching for it.

In that moment he felt hands seize his arms and pin them to his back. Immediately pain rocketed through him with an explosion of lights in his brain as Bear Kugan, a dim shape crouching before him, began to hammer him about the head and body with sledgehammer blows.

He had no wind, nor was there strength in his legs. He sagged, felt himself being pulled erect again, and the hail of punishing fists, halted briefly when consciousness and strength faltered, resumed.

A voice said, "Hell, Bear—he ain't feeling nothing. He's out on his feet."

There was no let up of the blows—shocking, staggering smashes to his head and body that left him without breath. Instinctively he endeavored to roll with the punches, absorb their force in the manner he'd learned to do.

"Come on, Bear—you've all but killed him now. Let's drag him off and get it over with. Me and Joe'll—"

Abruptly the voice broke off. Gunshots crackled from close by. The hands that gripped him released their hold on his arms, and the hammering fists stopped. As if in a dream Cameron felt himself sinking, drifting off into the shadows. Stubborn, he clung to his wavering senses.

Yells went up. There was cursing, the thud of a falling body, and then came the quick beat of horses racing away. Moments later Cameron felt himself being pulled upright.

"Them bastards—they sure worked him over! Good thing he's a tough one, or he'd be out cold."

The voice was distant, familiar, and the words spoken kept slipping in and out of his consciousness.

He recognized Ed Gorman's voice. "Man gets tough like that when he's in the pen for long. If he don't they're soon planting him in the boneyard. Hold him so's I can pour some of this whiskey down his gullet."

Cameron gulped as the liquor was forced into his mouth and down his throat. Gagging, his mind still not clear, pain throbbing throughout his body, he heard Turk Roper speak.

"It was that damned Kugan—him and two others. I didn't get no shot at him, but I fixed one of them that was holding the boss—fixed him for good."

"Reckon that red-eye done some good. He's sort of standing better—and his eyes've popped open . . . Here comes that lady now."

Lady . . . It was Darcy. Cameron recognized her voice when she asked how seriously hurt he was.

"Beat up plenty," Gorman replied, "but I expect he'll make it. We'll load him into your buggy like you want, then you best tote him to the doc, fast."

"I'll take of him—"

Cameron felt himself being half-carried, half-walked toward Darcy Mason's nearby vehicle. Assisted onto the seat, he slumped, still considerably dazed, and having no strength.

"Ma'am, you sure you ought to do this?" Turk Roper asked. "That bunch could still be hanging around, and if they catch you taking him to town—you being this fellow Mason's wife, and all that—it'll sure go hard for you."

"They won't see me," Darcy said. "I'll take him by a back way, and hide him somewhere—then get the doctor."

"You got a sawbones you can trust?" It was Ed Gorman again, his voice seemingly stronger than before. "Seems to me that husband of yours owns just about everybody around here."

There was a pause, and then Cameron heard the woman say, "You're probably right. I'd better not risk getting the doctor for him. There's a woman I know—he knows—who is good at nursing. I'll take him there."

John Cameron, only semiconscious, was vaguely aware of the hurried trip into town. But pain brought him to

full, jolting wakefulness when Darcy, halting in front of
Ketty Griffin's, and calling the girl to assist, got him out
of the buggy and into the house, where they laid him on
the bed.

"There was no other place I could think to take him
where he'd be safe," Cameron heard Darcy say.

His mind was now functioning near normal, thanks to
the goading of pain, and he was fully aware of the
situation, although so stiff and sore that any slight movement was agony. He found it difficult to speak, his lips
being badly swollen along with several loosened teeth,
while seeing was almost an impossibility, as his eyes
were little more than slits.

"I'm glad you brought him here—to me," Ketty replied.

"What about the doctor—do you think he'll need—"

"I don't think so," Ketty said in her quiet, self-assured
way. She was beginning to remove his clothing, had
already removed his boots, and now was working with the
buttons of his shirt. "I doubt there's any broken bones—
he's just terribly beaten. I'll give him a hot bath, put
salve on the cuts, and poultices on the swellings—"

"I can help—"

"No need," Ketty interrupted crisply. "I'm obliged to
you for bringing him here."

"But he could be in serious condition—internally, I
mean. He took a lot of punishment—I watched from the
edge of the yard. It was horrible! I was afraid he—"

Ketty paused, faced Darcy Mason. "Just leave it to me.
I grew up on a farm with five brothers, my pa—and no
mother. Spent most of my time, before I left, patching
them up, so I've had plenty of experience."

"I've heard how you've taken care of cowhands over at
the High Ridge, after they've been in a fight—"

"Don't you think it best you go?" Ketty broke in coolly. "Someone might see your buggy, suspect—"

"But I feel I should help—"

"You had your chance to help him three years ago," Ketty snapped, her voice rising, "but you failed him. Now let him be."

"So you can have him—all to yourself."

"Yes. You have a husband—go look after him. He'll be needing all the help he can get once John gets on his feet again."

"I'm sorry," Darcy murmured contritely. "I didn't mean for that to sound sharp. It's just that I'm so upset—that it hurt me so to see him standing there—being held by those two men while Bear Kugan kept hitting him—and John unable to fight back—"

"Where was John's crew?" Ketty asked, resuming the removal of Cameron's clothing. "There were three of them."

"They had their hands full with the rest of the riders Sid sent in to—well, to kill John."

Darcy shuddered at her own words. Ketty sighed heavily. "I guess it has started for sure now."

"I'm afraid so, and just how it will end is anybody's guess. There'll be a lot of men dead—I've lived with Sid long enough to know that his pride will never let him back down."

Ketty's voice was firm. "John Cameron won't back off, either; he believes in what he's trying to do, and nobody will ever change that . . . Now, thank you again for bringing him to me—and please go so I can take care of him."

"Of course," Darcy replied, and started to turn away. She hesitated. "We're not friends, Ketty, you should know that. I would never have brought John here if there had been any other place to go, but for his sake, not yours, I did. Good-bye."

Ketty murmured an unintelligible response, and when Darcy had left the house, she crossed to the door, and despite the mounting heat, closed and locked it. As she came back she found Cameron struggling to sit up.

"No," she said firmly, and pressed him to the bed again. "You're in no shape to go anywhere."

"Got to get to my ranch. Crew'll be needing me," he muttered.

"They need you alive, not dead, and that's what you'll be if you leave here and run into Bear Kugan or any other of the Muleshoe outfit. Finish taking off your clothes while I put some water to heating. A good soaking right away will take some of the soreness out of you."

Later, after a lengthy time hunched in a washtub of hot water, Cameron was back in the bed feeling considerably improved. He was still somewhat stiff, and where Kugan's rock-hard fists had connected there was yet a good bit of tenderness; but on the whole Ketty Griffin's treatment of near scalding water baths, continual massaging, and applications of ointment was doing him much good. Only his eyes seemed to resist her efforts, and when night came—despite the poultices she had pressed upon them—he found that it was all he could do to see through the slits between his puffed lids.

"Seems I'm going to have to stay here till morning," he said when Ketty brought him a cup of steaming black coffee. "I'm hoping Gorman and the others are all right."

"They will be. They drove Kugan and the other Muleshoe men off—killed two, I think."

"Where'd you hear that?"

Ketty shrugged, settled back in one of the rockers. "From Darcy. She saw it all from the edge of your yard—so she claimed." The woman paused, then: "What was she doing there?"

Cameron studied her soft, lovely features through his hooded eyes. He had heard a good bit of the conversation that had passed between her and Darcy, and had a fair knowledge of what all had happened while he was slipping in and out of full consciousness.

"Came to warn me that Kugan and a bunch of Mason's riders were on the way. Were to wipe us out. Just did get her out of sight when they showed up." Cameron's voice trailed off, and a hardness came into his features noticeable despite the swellings and discolorations. "Know exactly now where things stand—and what I have to do."

"Why didn't Darcy leave when you helped her to hide? Why did she continue to hang around? Seems to me she was taking a big chance to stay. If Sid ever finds out—"

"Hell, I don't know why she did! Told her to go on—anyway, what difference does it make?" Cameron asked, nettled by Ketty's persistent dwelling on the matter.

"None, I suppose, only it looks to me as if her marriage to Sid Mason's not worth much. Maybe she—she's hoping to—"

When Ketty hesitated over her words, Cameron stirred angrily. "Hoping I'd start up with her again—that what you're trying to say?"

"Yes, I suppose so—"

"You can forget that," Cameron said, voice a bit sharp. "Darcy's out of my life—has been for three years. I'm obliged to her for warning me that Kugan and the others were coming—and for bringing me here, but that's all it amounts to. If she hadn't let us know we'd probably have been in big trouble, and I owe her for that. But this is only the first verse, far as me and Mason's concerned. Next one I'll do the singing."

Ketty was silent for a long breath. Then, "What about us, John?"

"Us?"

"Yes, where do we stand—you and me?"

"Thought I'd made that clear. Just give me time to get this thing with Mason over and done with, then I'll be asking you to be my wife."

Ketty's head came up at that, and a smile parted her lips.

"I won't have much to offer, but I'll be selling those steers of mine to a buyer in Silver City for seven dollars a head—and I should have most of that left over after paying off my crew, feeding them and such—but it'll be enough for us to get started on. That what you wanted to hear?"

"Yes, John—that's what I was hoping you'd say. But—"

"But what?"

"I'd feel better about it all if we could just pack up and leave right now. They almost killed you! Next time it could turn out different."

"Could, no denying that, but probably won't. I'll be the one who makes the next move—me and the three men who've thrown in with me. Sid Mason's bunch will never catch us with our guard down again."

"How can you keep him from it? He's got a dozen men to send after you—two dozen if necessary. And he knows the only help you'll have are the three men you've got working for you. How can you expect to buck odds like that?"

"Easier for four men to move about than a big party of

a dozen or more . . . What about Lige Davidson, and the others that Mason crooked—you think I'll be getting any help from them?"

"Doesn't sound good. Did get a chance to talk to Lige again, and he did say he'd do some thinking about it. Nobody else has been around . . . I'm going to have to go to work. I want your promise that you'll stay in bed. If you do, and we have good luck, you'll be up and around by morning. I'll lock the door."

Cameron nodded, motioned at his belt and gun lying on the table. He had dropped the weapon during the fight with Bear Kugan, and guessed one of the members of his crew had recovered it and put it back in his holster.

"Expect I'd better have my iron handy—"

Ketty brought the weapon to him, and as she drew close, he caught her by the arms and pulled her close. Ignoring his aches, and despite his swollen, pain-filled lips, he kissed her solidly.

"That's for being you," he managed, "and for being my wife real soon. Want you to know that's the way I feel about it."

Ketty smiled happily. "It can't be too soon to suit me," she said, and turned to go.

Ketty was awake and up ahead of him preparing breakfast that next morning. Pulling himself to a sitting position under protest of every muscle in his body, he swung his legs off the side of the bed. Ketty, at the stove, paused to watch.

"Can you see?" she asked, when that maneuver had been accomplished.

Cameron glanced about, nodded. "Better than last night,

for sure. Whatever it was you doctored me with done a lot of good."

"Was those hot baths, mostly—and that ointment," she answered as he began to draw on his clothes. "I don't know what's in it—something from a plant that grows out on the plains, I think. And, of course, those poultices helped your eyes."

Dressed, Cameron got shakily to his feet, and slowly and carefully tested his arms, legs, and hands.

"Pretty good, considering," he said, and started toward the woman. "If you—"

A loud pounding on the door brought Cameron up short. He turned, pain dragging at his face at the sudden movement, and dropping a hand onto the pistol now hanging at his hip, nodded to Ketty.

"See who it is—"

The woman crossed the room, unlocked the panel, and drew it back. Ed Gorman looked in, flushed and smiling. Behind him, equally joyous, were Turk Roper and Virg Bratton.

"Howdy, ma'am! Howdy, boss!" Gorman boomed.

Concern immediately filled Cameron, as the three men, all showing the effects of considerable liquor, filed into the room.

"Sure mighty pleased you ain't no worse off than you are," Gorman said. "Sure was a pitiable mess when that lady loaded you up and headed for town."

"Glad to see none of you got yourself shot yesterday. How is—"

"Was them Muleshoes that got themselves shot!" Virg Bratton declared. "Put two of them in the graveyard, and winged a couple more. We been celebrating what we done to them down at that little one-horse saloon, the

Cottonwood—letting everybody know that them Muleshoe waddies ain't so tough—"

"Celebrating—all night?" Cameron said, the concern in him turning quickly to fear. "You saying you've been in town all night?"

"Mostly," Gorman replied. "We hung around the ranch till dang nigh midnight, waiting to see if any of them'd come back—but none of them did. Had all they wanted, I expect."

"So we come on in to town," Virg added, "and had us a humdinger of a time! Was wishing all the time you was there."

"We're on our way back now," Gorman explained. "Figured we'd drop by, leave you your horse so's you'd have something to ride when you got ready to come home. Weren't exactly sure where you'd be, but I had a hunch this here's where the lady would be bringing you. Now if—"

Cameron had pulled on his hat, and was already moving for the doorway. "We best get to the ranch fast," he said in a tight voice. "No telling what they've done to the place if they came by and found nobody there!"

CHAPTER 12

~~~~~~

Cameron led the way back, not following the usual road to the J-Bar-C, but cutting directly across the hills and flats. The first few miles in the saddle, with the buckskin moving at a good lope, were sheer misery to him, but the soreness in his hard-muscled body gradually wore off, and coupled with the anxiety that gripped him, was soon forgotten. His vision was something else; his eyes were still badly swollen, as was his face, and he had difficulty in seeing well—but that, too, he ignored.

"If that bunch has gone and done what you're a'fearing," Gorman said, kneeing his mount in close to Cameron's, "why I sure—"

"If they haven't, it'll be the luckiest day we've ever lived," Cameron retorted, his voice sharp. There was a grimness to him, an almost tangible force that had quickly transferred itself to the others.

Gorman wagged his head, swore. "We sure wasn't thinking much—going off like we did. I should've known better."

Cameron agreed silently. It hadn't occurred to him while he was being administered to by Ketty Griffin, and later while resting and recovering under her care, that the crew would ride off, leaving the ranch unprotected. But they had, and while he had no definite knowledge yet that Muleshoe had struck in their absence, destroying what few possessions he owned and leveling what remained of his ranch, he felt it was almost a certainty.

Sid Mason would have been like a wild man when he learned that Kugan and the men with him—sent to do a job—had failed. Odds were a hundred to one that he'd not let matters rest for long, but would send Bear, with plenty of help, back to do things up right.

"Can smell smoke," Virg Bratton called out as they rode down off a ridge and entered the swale where the J-Bar-C lay.

There was too much timber and brush to see the place from the ridge, but the odor was strong on the early morning breeze, and John Cameron knew his worst fears were true even before they broke out of the thick growth on the slope and looked out over a narrow flat at what had once been John Cameron's dream.

"There ain't nothing left," Gorman muttered as they closed up and side by side stared at the smoky scene.

The bunkhouse had been torn apart. Of little flammable material, its walls had been pulled down, and fire set to its contents. The brush corral was gone—was now just a pile of graying ashes spinning in the passing wind.

"What'll we do now?" Bratton wondered as they continued their slow approach.

"Why, we just get us some more grub and such, and start over," Gorman answered. "We can't let them get—"

"No," Cameron said in a harsh voice as they halted

before what had been the bunkhouse and their living quarters. The only recognizable items from it were the two stoves lying bottom up in the charred embers—legs poking rigidly into the air—like bloated pigs. "I'm done."

"Done?" Gorman echoed in surprise. "You mean you're quitting?"

"No—done with trying to get things set—get ready," Cameron replied, suppressed anger hardening his voice. "Was a fool thing to do—I can see that now. Ought to have known Sid Mason wouldn't hold off, but would begin cracking down on me right after I got off that stage. If I'd been half smart I would've been the one to make the first move."

"Been a mite hard to do alone," Turk said doubtfully. "Ain't meaning to sell you short none—you've already proved you ain't one to tangle with—but that Muleshoe bunch is plenty mean and tough, and there's a lot of them. What's more, there ain't no lawman around here that'll give you a hand."

"I realize that, but I should've taken my chances. All I've done is waste time and money, get the hell beat out of me a couple of times—and put the whip handle into Mason's hand."

"Maybe so," Gorman said, brushing his hat to the back of his head, "but I misdoubt you're a man to bury a dog before it's dead. What are you aiming to do now?"

"I'm going to give Muleshoe a taste of their own cooking—set fire to it."

Virg Bratton uttered a sound of pleasure, and grinned broadly. Roper nodded approval, while Ed Gorman rubbed his palms together gleefully.

"That there's just what that Mason fellow's got coming—a good burning out!"

Cameron, unsmiling, raised a hand for silence. "Want to say that I appreciate your standing by me, but you don't need to mix yourselves in my troubles any longer. From here on it will be a showdown—a fight to a finish."

There were a few moments of silence, and then Roper drawled, "You don't see nobody backing off, do you?"

"No, but you know the kind of odds I'm bucking, and I wouldn't fault you none, any of you, for drawing what pay you've got coming and clearing out."

Again there was quiet, broken this time by Ed Gorman. "I reckon we'll wait and do our pay-collecting after we've helped you square up with this Sid Mason—sure wouldn't want to miss any fun. When're you figuring to put on this little fandango?"

"Tonight," Cameron said, and paused as Ketty Griffin came into view.

The girl was driving a buggy, one rented from Charlie Sweeney, he supposed. Ketty appeared worried, and Cameron, coming down off his saddle when the woman pulled to a stop nearby, stepped in close to the vehicle.

She considered the blackened ruins in shocked silence. Cameron smiled tautly. "They done a good job—wiped me out completely."

Ketty turned to him. "I'm sorry, John," she said heavily. "Maybe if you—"

"The real war begins tonight," he said. "When we get through Sid Mason will know what it's like to get burnt out—and I reckon it'll be a right good start at driving him from the valley."

Ketty's face was calm, her eyes sober. "You're going to set fire to Muleshoe?"

"What we'll do just as soon as dark settles in. Now there's no use staying here—nothing left to stay for. We'll hole up at the old Hanlon place—that's a cabin a couple of miles south of here."

"I know where it is—we had a picnic there once," Ketty said.

"I figured you did, but I wanted the boys to know how to find it in case we get split up tonight. Guess we might as well ride over there now, and lay low for the rest of the day."

Ketty nodded. "You'll be needing something to eat. I'll go fix a basket, and bring it to you as soon as I can."

"That'll be fine," Cameron said, stepping back from the buggy. "Just be careful you're not followed. I don't want anything busting loose until tonight."

"I'll take care," Ketty said, and slapping the horse's rump with the lines, she cut the buggy about and headed for town.

It was late, well onto midnight, when John Cameron and his three-men crew left the Hanlon place and struck for Muleshoe. He took them not by the road, fearing a chance encounter with some of Mason's men, but along a trail that cut a winding trace through groves of trees, stands of thick brush, and scattered rock.

They moved slowly, but steadily. Cameron was fully aware each minute of his aches and pains, and as they drew near Mason's sprawling spread, his caution increased. He warned the other men with him to be alert for any indication that Sid Mason, expecting retaliation, might have guards stationed around the ranch proper.

Overhead the sky was a vast, dark blanket splattered with multisized diamonds and a crescent moon. A light wind, cool at that hour, fanned their faces as it rustled the dry leaves about them. Coyotes were barking back and forth on the distant slopes of the Navajos—their disharmony a forlorn sound in the stillness of the night.

"Sure is quiet," Virg Bratton murmured. "Things are just right for doing what we aim to."

"Won't never be a better time," Gorman agreed. "Can fill your belly with revenge tonight, Cameron."

Revenge . . . John Cameron gave the word thought. He had not considered what he was doing an act of revenge, but rather one of justice. Could his thinking be wrong? Deep inside him, pushing him relentlessly on was that determination to break Sid Mason and drive the man from the Red Rock Valley country; was it, in reality, in the spirit of vengeance? Was he fooling himself, and trying to fool others, when he insisted what he had undertaken was not revenge?

Cameron shrugged, endeavoring to shake off his disturbing thoughts. He didn't believe it was, and further endorsed such conviction by telling himself that he would gain nothing personally by what he was doing; when it was all over and he found himself still alive, it would not be he who benefited from Sid Mason's departure, but those whom Muleshoe had wronged.

Was that vengeance? Or was it simply retribution, vested in him by circumstances, catching up with Mason? He mulled that about in his mind for several moments, and then stirred impatiently in his saddle. He guessed it didn't matter, and he really didn't give a damn. All that counted was driving Mason from the land he had taken by any means necessary, force included, and returning it to its rightful owners.

Cameron looked ahead through the pale darkness. The swale across which they were crossing had begun to lift toward a wide saddle created by the juncture of two hills. Beyond it lay the houses and other buildings of Muleshoe.

"When we top out that ridge," he said, pointing, "we'll be there. Best we go double easy from here on—and stay in close. We'll do our planning once we're where we can get the lay of the place."

They moved on, staying in the wide meadow that now rolled off to the west of a large grove, but keeping near the trees where their chances of passing unnoticed were good. The slope to the saddle was fairly steep, but they did not press their horses to reach the summit, and when they finally did all four mounts were blowing for wind.

"That's it," Cameron said, pointing down into a large hollow in the center of which were a number of buildings. "Big place on the right's the main house. One where the crew bunks is off to its left. That's a barn on beyond it, near all the corrals."

"Ain't nobody up," Roper said, studying the structure. "This ought to be real easy."

"Maybe've got somebody setting around in the dark places," Gorman said. "Kind of hard to think they ain't expecting us."

"Seems we would have run into a guard before now if Sid had figured that way. Leaving me in the shape Kugan and his two friends did, and burning my place to the ground, he may think he's seen the last of me."

"Man sure has got a powerful good opinion of himself," Roper commented. "Kind of like to meet him, sort of face to face."

"Expect we best leave that pleasure for the boss," Gorman said.

"I don't much give a damn one way or the other," Cameron said. "All I want is Sid Mason gone. Only score

I'd like to settle personally is with Bear Kugan—and I aim to if I get the chance."

"You ain't in such good shape to tackle Bear—"

"Maybe so, but I will if I get the chance."

Turk Roper shifted in his saddle, hung one leg over the horn. "If we're doing some picking and choosing, I'm staking my claim on that marshal—Stanwyck, he calls himself these days."

"All yours far as I'm concerned, Turk," Gorman said.

"Same here," Virg Bratton echoed, and when Cameron made no comment, added, "That jake with you, boss?"

"Already said I didn't want any more killing than necessary—none at all if we can get out of it."

"Already been a couple that we know of—maybe even more," Gorman said. "Just can't have bacon without slaughtering the pig."

"I realize that, and Turk, if you've got something to settle with Nate Stanwyck—or whatever his real name is—I don't aim to stand in your way. Only thing I'm asking is that you wait till we get this business of mine finished."

"He ain't likely to be around Mason's place tonight," Bratton said.

"I ain't expecting him to be," Roper said, "but tomorrow's another day."

"Can do what you please tomorrow," Cameron said. He threw his glance again into the hollow below. Lamplight now gleamed in a window of the crew's quarters where, for one reason or another, someone had roused. "Best we get started. Ed, you and Turk circle around and take care of the bunkhouse. Virg and me will handle the rest."

"Any special way you're planning to do this job? I

know we done talked it over, but I like to be dang sure I'm doing what a man wants me to do."

Cameron nodded to Gorman. "Any way that will work. Be sure you get a good fire going—there's plenty of dry brush around that you can use. I want every building and shed on the place burning by the time we hit for the hills—they're about a quarter mile or so west of here. You'll find plenty of trees and rocks to lose yourself in. When you're certain you're not being followed, light out for the Hanlon place."

"How'll we know when you and Virg are all set?" Gorman asked. "We don't want to get the jump on you."

"You go ahead, leave that to me. When I see you two have your fire going, Virg and me'll make our move."

Gorman and Roper, again square in his saddle, swung quietly away, angling off into the deep shadows into the direction of the crew's quarters. When they were no longer visible, Cameron spoke softly to Bratton, and together they moved off, taking a route that would bring them in at the end of Muleshoe's main house. From there Cameron figured he could see Turk Roper and Gorman when they put a torch to the brush and weeds they would throw against the low walled structure.

At that moment he would apply a match to the pile of tinder he and Virg Bratton would have placed along the blind side of Mason's house. The flames, in both instances being where they would not be immediately visible to anyone on the ranch, should have a good start by the time discovery came.

It was a slow, tense, half-hour ride from where they had halted to the weedy area behind the ranch house. Halting at a squat juniper tree, they dismounted and secured the horses. Moving about quietly, they gathered

up as much dry brush as they could carry, and continuing
on through the half dark, placed it along the foot of the
frame structure which rested on foot-high mounds of
rock.

Motioning to Virg to put his armload of brush well
under the house in the open spaces between the founda-
tions, Cameron crossed to the corner of the structure and
looked off over the hardpack to the bunkhouse.

The window, one to the south, still showed a square of
yellow light. A frown pulled at Cameron's bruised and
battered features. It could be that some of the crew were
rousing to do nighthawk duty with Mason's herds, but
generally such changes were made earlier. More than
likely it was one of the men having trouble sleeping—or
perhaps fighting a bellyache or the effects of too much
whiskey; or it might be one who had been wounded in the
encounter that previous day.

At that moment Cameron caught sight of Turk Roper
and Gorman—two vague, indefinite figures moving slowly
about the near end of the bunkhouse as they piled brush
and other inflammables against its timber walls.

"Can see a lantern hanging there at the end of the
porch," Bratton said in a low voice, at once catching
Cameron's attention. "How about me getting it and pouring coal oil on the side of the house?"

Cameron followed Virg Bratton's pointing finger. The
lantern was but a dozen strides away at the corner of the
ranch house.

"Be a good idea—but go quiet. Not sure about that
light across the yard there in the bunkhouse. Somebody
just might come out—"

"Well, somebody's coming!" Bratton warned softly,
freezing after he'd moved off a stride or two.

"Get low," Cameron said, dropping to a crouch in the deep shadows alongside the house.

Four riders . . . They came up fast on the road that led from town, and when they reached the edge of the hardpack, pulled in noticeably, evidently hoping to avoid wakening those who were sleeping. Crossing the yard with horses at a walk, they entered the corral next to the bunkhouse and turned their animals loose, still saddled and bridled. Wheeling, they returned to the low-roofed structure that housed the crew, and disappeared inside.

"Bunch coming back from town," Virg commented, and continued his mission to get the lantern.

Cameron's attention was again on the bunkhouse. Ed Gorman and Roper had faded into the darkness when the riders had come into the yard. For a time there was no sign of the pair as they apparently waited until all was quiet inside the building before resuming their chore.

One of the horses in the corral blew noisily, and another window showed light in the crew's quarters. Virg returned with the lantern, and unscrewing the filler cap, began to splash oil along the edge of the house and onto the brush piled under it.

"I'm saving a little," he said when the job was done. "Can use it on some of them sheds."

Abruptly both windows in the bunkhouse went dark. Cameron drew the oilskin packet in which he carried matches from his pocket, and handed several to Bratton. Selecting one for himself, he glanced toward the bunkhouse. He could see movement—only one man. It was Gorman, he thought. Evidently Turk had gone on to another of the structures, and was preparing to torch it.

Time dragged slowly by, moments filled with tension, with the clicking of insects in the weeds, the loud chirping of a cricket somewhere under the house. An owl hooted off in the distance, and one of the horses in the corral stamped wearily.

And then a small flame flared in the darkness near the crew's quarters. Ed Gorman's hunched shape was briefly silhouetted as he touched his lucifer to the brush piled against the building. Farther on a second flame broke the night alongside the barn: Turk Roper.

"Now," Cameron said, dragging the match he held across the seat of his pants. Holding it for several seconds to make certain the flame was strong, he tossed it into the oil-soaked brush. He turned to Virg Bratton. "Soon as your fire's going, get to your horse. If we're lucky we'll have time to set a couple more blazes."

Down near the barn a dog had begun to bark furiously. Cameron pivoted, seeing Bratton's end of the brush pile spring into vivid, dancing life—and pulled up short. The fire at the end of the bunkhouse had gone out. He could see Gorman bending close to its wall attempting to start it again. Farther over the side of the barn was already a sheet of leaping flames. Roper had evidently spotted a lantern, too, and made good use of it.

The fire at the bunkhouse caught. Gorman hesitated for several moments, making certain that it would not again go out, and then as the yellow flames shot upward amid boiling puffs of smoke, he dropped back out of sight.

"Let's go—we'll have Muleshoe hired help all over us in a couple of minutes if we don't move!" Cameron said, a surging exhilaration filling him. "Head toward—"

His words broke off. Virg Bratton had already gone.

CHAPTER 13

~~~~~~

Cameron swore, whirled, and ran to where the buckskin was tethered. There were now three separate fires going, the main house, the crew's quarters, and the barn. It would not be long now before everyone on Muleshoe was aroused.

Reaching the gelding, Cameron yanked the reins free and swung up into the saddle. As he wheeled the buckskin about he heard the pound of hoofs on the hardpack. He glanced toward the sound, saw Virg Bratton, bent low over his horse, racing across the yard for a wagon shed where half a dozen vehicles were parked. As Cameron came into the yard himself Cameron saw Bratton pause, smash the lantern he was carrying against the side of the shed, and throw a lighted match into the splatter of oil. As flames shot upward, Virg let out with a wild yell and spurred off into the murky haze near the barn.

A gunshot shattered the crackling sound of burning wood, and Cameron, now skirting the yard, felt the breath of a bullet. Surprised, as there were still no Muleshoe men in evidence, he looked over his shoulder. Sid Mason was standing on the porch of the ranch house, the lower end of which was a roaring mass of flames. Cursing, Cameron brought up his weapon for a quick shot, hesitated when he saw Darcy clad in a white robe appear in the doorway. At once he lowered the forty-five, and raking the gelding with his spurs, rushed on toward the darkness beyond the barn where Gorman and the others appeared to be.

He veered sharply. Four more riders swept into the yard, also coming from town. They were close—so close that Cameron recognized Bear Kugan, the new rider Ben Lancaster, and the Leavitts, Dan and Curly.

Instantly Kugan whipped out his pistol and threw a shot at Cameron, but he fired too hastily and the bullet was wide. Cameron replied with two quick shots in the general direction of the riders, all of whom now had their guns out, and rushed on through the smoke-filled lurid glare.

Men were coming out of the bunkhouse into the yard, drawn not only by the rattle of gunfire, but driven so by the heat of the fire hungrily consuming the dry wood. All were in various degrees of dress—some in drawers, but having pulled on their boots; others had taken time to don pants, a few also included their shirts and hats, while all were wearing footgear. To a man, however, they had their weapons, and at once began to shoot at the shadowy figures beyond the flare of flames, not knowing if their targets were friend or foe.

Cameron, ignoring the bedlam, hurried along the rear of the bunkhouse, and curved into the weed-covered area beyond the barn—now a roaring bulk of fire from which several Muleshoe men were laboring frantically to remove a number of horses and mules. Drifting smoke was now making it difficult to see, but Cameron could hear riders whipping back and forth across the yard, and once Sid Mason's voice came to him calling for more men to get mounted.

A rider materialized suddenly on Cameron's left, bringing him quickly about, his pistol up. It was Turk Roper.

"Where's Gorman?" Cameron shouted, struggling to keep the buckskin in hand.

"Don't know," Roper replied. "We got the fires to going, then I went off to fix the barn. Ain't seen the old man since. Kind of got me worried some."

"He's around here somewhere then," Cameron said, slipping from the saddle and handing the reins of the nervous gelding to Roper. "Hold this damn horse while I have a look."

Keeping close to the back of the bunkhouse, blazing furiously on both its north end and front side, Cameron worked his way to the corner. Gorman, crouched low, a torch in his hand, was moving toward a small shed standing a few paces into the yard.

"Ed—here!" Cameron shouted. For the older man to expose himself was not only dangerous, but unnecessary as the fires, shooting forth flaming embers, were spreading rapidly on their own.

Gorman hesitated, then took two more strides and hurled the burning torch against the wall of the shed. A man in the yard, catching the flare of a new fire, saw Gorman and opened up on him. The bullets were low, dug into the dust at Ed Gorman's feet. Other Muleshoe men took up the shooting, and shortly lead was filling the hazy air.

Cameron, weapon reloaded, crouched beside Gorman

and returned the fire. Virg Bratton, appearing suddenly in the murk, rode straight into the yard and began to throw his shots at the cluster of men standing in front of the bunkhouse. They were well out in the open, the fire having driven them away from the structure and its protection.

Roper, handicapped by Cameron's fractious horse, came up from the direction of the doomed barn. Curving in close to Cameron, he shouted, "Take this damned nag!" and flinging the lines at Cameron, rushed on into the yard to side Bratton.

The buckskin was frantic. The hammering of guns, the crackling and heat of the fires, the shouting, and the thick choking smoke were turning him wild. At that moment Cameron recalled Charlie Sweeney's admonition that the gelding was a bit gun-shy.

"Only a mite," Cameron muttered, drawing the animal's head down firmly in hopes of quieting him some.

Abruptly Gorman, now mounted, rode up, a broad grin on his soot-streaked face. "Sure having us some fun, ain't we?"

Cameron nodded, and managing to get back on the buckskin, looked into the yard. Several mounted men were milling about—at least a dozen, he figured. All they needed was to get organized, after which they would begin a systematic search for the raiders who had destroyed Muleshoe—and that would certainly occur as soon as Sid Mason or Bear Kugan took charge.

"Let's get out of here!" Cameron shouted. "We've done all the damage we could."

Gorman continued to smile and throw shots into the yard. Cameron looked about for Roper and Virg Bratton, saw the younger man wheeling in and out of the hanging smoke, and disorganized riders. The group in front of the crew's quarters had now broken up, and a smaller party had collected near the first of the corrals. At that moment another of Mason's men came suddenly out from behind one of the blazing sheds. He spilled from his saddle as Turk Roper wheeled out of the fire-tinted gloom directly in front of him. Roper dropped him with a single, quick shot.

Cameron could vaguely see other Muleshoe men down on the hardpack. Two lay near the bunkhouse hitch rack, another was sprawled a short distance farther on. There would be others, he knew, as he worked deeper into the yard, endeavoring to locate Bratton and Roper. He looked again to the main house, having a sudden remembrance of seeing Darcy there on the porch with her husband. The entire front of the structure was now in flames, and there was no sign of either. Hopefully Darcy had gotten away from the stricken building and found safety in the shadows beyond it.

"Turk! Virg!"

Cameron raised his voice to its limit. There were far too many Muleshoe men mounted now for them to tarry longer. Roper and Bratton heard him, turned to look. Cameron beckoned. In that same brief bit of time three Muleshoe riders came pounding in from somewhere near the corrals, guns booming through the confusion of smoke, heat, and glare.

Cameron shouted a warning, and spun to meet the rush. Bullets whispered past him, one striking the metal horn of his saddle and richocheting shrilly off into the violent night. Gorman abruptly appeared, his horse crowding in on the nervous buckskin, immediately causing him to rear and pitch. Abandoning the use of his gun, Cameron fought the gelding but had little luck as the animal continued to shy deeper into the yard.

Retreat into the brushy hills as originally planned was now out of the question; through circumstances they had delayed too long. The only route open to them was past the bunkhouse which would expose them to a cross fire of the riders gathered at each end of the hardpack. But there was no alternative; it would have to be done that way if they were to get out at all; to stay and fight against such odds would be fatal.

"Virg—Turk—this way!"

Cameron raked the buckskin savagely with his spurs, got him headed toward the flaming bunkhouse. Gorman and Turk Roper swerved in behind him, maintaining a continual fire at the men in the yard. Virg Bratton, seeing them racing away, came about sharply and followed. Cameron glanced back to see if all three men were coming. He nodded, satisfied, and then a curse ripped from his lips. Virg Bratton had abruptly stiffened. The young rider remained rigid for a long breath, swayed, and then toppled to the ground, his body bouncing lifelessly.

Turk Roper halted instantly. Cameron saw the gunman take deliberate aim at the man who had apparently fired the shot. The pistol bucked in Roper's hand, and the Muleshoe rider twisted about and fell from his saddle.

Cameron forced the buckskin back into the yard, and leaped to the ground beside Bratton. Turk Roper and Ed Gorman wheeled in close, their guns hammering. Cameron rolled Bratton over onto his back and knelt over him. Virg was dead—there was nothing to be done for him, and with Mason's men now together and starting to move in, there wasn't even time to load the young rider's body onto his horse and take it away for burial. Pivoting, Cameron hurried back to the buckskin, seized the reins that were being held by Gorman, and mounting, brought his own gun into play.

Leading the way, Cameron struck for the shadows at the end of the hardpack beyond the flames of the bunkhouse which were beginning to exhaust themselves. They reached the darkness, and plunged into its protective cover with bullets snapping all about them. The buckskin, free now of the frightening pandemonium in the yard, lowered his head and stretched into a fast run. Cameron looked back over his shoulder at Roper and Gorman.

"Scatter—into the brush!" he shouted. "You know where to go!".

It was a long, nerve-wracking space to the first outcropping of scrub trees, rocks, and rank growth, but the half-crazed buckskin reached them in full stride, not slowing even when the stiff, resisting branches met him head on and scraped along his flanks as he thundered by. The horse was frightened to the point of insanity, and Cameron, hearing the shouts and crashing sounds of pursuit, let him have his reckless way.

Cameron caught a flashing glimpse of Gorman and Roper in the dappled half-light among the trees off to his left, and then quickly lost them in the heavy brush. Yells still filled the cool night, along with the crash of guns and the dull thunk of bullets driving into close-by trees, or the clipping sound as they cut through leaves.

Cameron recoiled suddenly as a gun flamed in the night only short yards off to his right. Even as surging, burning pain told him he had been hit, he triggered his own weapon, and grinned with satisfaction when he saw the rider fall from the saddle. The buckskin, more frightened than ever, pounded on, whipping in and out of the brush and trees, gradually drawing away from the Muleshoe riders. A thread of relief ran through John Cameron when that became apparent; the slope up which they were fleeing had become steeper, and he knew the gelding, for all his fear, could not continue the pace at which he was running much longer. He would have to halt. He'd have a look at his wound—in the upper, fleshy part of his left arm—at that time, and see how badly he was hurt.

But the buckskin, wracked with fear, was not ready to quit. He continued his headlong climb for another quarter mile before Cameron, now feeling pain from the bullet wound, was able to slow him down and get him under control.

Cameron did not bring the horse to a halt, but allowed him to proceed at a slow walk in a weaving pattern through the heavy growth. There was no more shooting now, but he could trace the movements of Sid Mason's men by their shouting as they worked through their way across the slope.

Shortly Cameron came to a shallow bowl, one well hidden by mountain mahogany and other bushy growth, and immediately turned the winded gelding into it. He'd take a few minutes and breathe the horse, and at the same time do what he could for the wound in his arm; it didn't appear to be a serious injury although it was bleeding considerably.

Remaining in the saddle, he pulled out his bandanna and wrapped it about his bloody upper arm. That should suffice until he got to the Hanlon place; there, with the help of Roper or Ed Gorman or perhaps Ketty Griffin, he'd get the wound tended to properly.

Cameron glanced around. It was growing light, and he

wanted to be well out of the area before darkness had faded. Pulling on the reins, he raised the buckskin's head, cut him about, and using his spurs, rode the weary horse up out of the hollow. Glancing about to get his bearings, Cameron struck a straight-line course for the Hanlon place.

CHAPTER 14

Despite the steadily bleeding wound in his arm, John Cameron took care in reaching the Hanlon place, fearing that one or more of Sid Mason's Muleshoe men could have seen him moving through the trees and followed.

Circling the old shack at a safe distance, he halted in the brush well beyond, and sat out a good quarter hour while his arm throbbed and bled. Finally convinced no one had been on his trail, he made his way to the shack.

Leaving the buckskin hidden in the brush immediately behind the place; Cameron crossed to the entrance of the weathered old structure. Two horses were picketed off in the thick growth at the side, he noted, one of which Turk Roper had been riding; the other he assumed was Ed Gorman's.

Rapping softly on the door to announce his presence, Cameron pushed it open and stepped inside. Turk Roper was sitting on a bench affixed to the opposite wall, and standing in the center of the room was Ketty Griffin.

A glad sound of relief came from the girl's throat when she saw him, and at once she hurried forward.

"Oh, John! I was beginning to—you're hurt! You've been shot!" she cried in a rush of words.

Turk Roper glanced up, frowning. Cameron, his good arm about the woman, the other hanging limply at his side, shook his head.

"Don't think it amounts to much. Bone's not broken . . . Where's Gorman?"

Turk's shoulders stirred. "Ain't seen him—not since we was riding out of that yard."

"Thought he was with you," Cameron said.

"Was," the gunman said. He was wiping at his pistol with a bandanna, removing any dirt and accumulation of burnt powder residue from its mechanism. "We split up when that bunch got to crowding us . . . Aim to go looking for him pretty quick if he don't show up . . . I'm getting low on cartridges."

Ketty had led Cameron to an overturned nail keg in one corner of the room where a window let in a shaft of early morning light. Motioning for him to be seated, she removed his jacket and shirt to expose the wound.

"Seen that fellow Mason come out of the house and take a shot at you," Roper said in a flat voice. "Seen you throw down on him—but you didn't fire. Been wondering why. Could've ended this ruckus right there and then."

"His wife was standing close by him. Was scared I might hit her."

Ketty paused in the act of cleaning his wound with a bit of cloth wet from the water in the canteen she had brought along with food the previous day.

Roper shrugged. "Maybe if you hadn't done that Virg

wouldn't be lying back there dead," he said. "Could go
for Gorman, too."

Ketty resumed working on the wound, now pouring
whiskey into the torn flesh, and after Cameron had ceased
writhing, applying an ointment of some kind.

"Whereabouts was you when you got hit?" Roper
continued. /He had finished cleaning his weapon, had
thrust it back into its holster. Outside it was now full
daylight with the sun already beginning its climb into the
clean blue of the heavens.

"Was going up that slope west of the yard—had just
seen you and Gorman making it off to my left. Reckon I
can thank the buckskin for getting me out of there fast.
He goes crazy where there's a lot of yelling and shooting
around him."

"Good thing he's that way, I reckon. The woods was
lousy with them Muleshoe gunnies . . . You spare a few
cartridges?"

Ketty had finished dressing and binding the wound in
Cameron's arm, and stepped back. She studied him briefly
for a few moments, and then closing her lips tightly,
collected the few medical articles she had thoughtfully
brought along with the basket of food and returned them
to their box. Cameron, in compliance with Turk Roper's
request, began to thumb shells from his belt—half a
dozen or so—and hand them to the gunman.

"Can give you half of what I've got left," he said. "Got
to figure a way to get a box or two. No way of knowing
what we'll be up against now."

Roper pushed the brass cartridges into the empty loops
in his belt. "Yep, I expect we'll be needing a lot more'n
we've got. That fellow Mason ain't going to let things ride
now."

"I can go to town to get some," Ketty volunteered.

Cameron frowned. "Not sure you'd be safe."

"Reason I came on horseback, and not in a buggy. Can ride the back trails where nobody'd see me. You be all right while I'm gone—your arm, I mean?"

"No worry there—"

"You're not figuring to leave here?"

"No—"

"That's a relief. You're in no shape to do any riding—not for a few hours anyway. If you'll promise to stay right here, eat something, and get some sleep, I'll go after some shells for you."

Cameron smiled tightly, brushed at his still swollen eyes. "Way I feel right now, nothing short of damnation will get me outside. Go to Walton's and tell Harry you want two boxes of forty-fives," he added and handed her a gold eagle.

Ketty dropped the coin into a pocket and started for the door. She looked back at Roper. "I'll be obliged if you'll see that he stays put. I'm afraid he'll—"

"Reckon you'll have to just take his word for it, ma'am," he said, getting leisurely to his feet. "I'm going out to look for the old man—for Gorman."

Turk rode due northeast, the direction in which Muleshoe lay, and the area where he had last seen his longtime friend. It would be a blind search, he knew; Gorman could be anywhere within a ten- or twelve-mile square—dead or badly wounded.

Likely wounded, Roper decided, glancing upward at a flock of crows straggling by overhead. He couldn't visualize Gorman dead; the old man, as he affectionately thought of him, was much too wise to let that happen to him.

In all the years they'd knocked around together, following the trails, wandering from town to town—large, small, and mere wide places along the road where the only thing to be found was a saloon—Ed Gorman had always been the cagey, careful one. To think now that a bullet from the gun of a man neither of them knew, and with whom they actually had no quarrel, had caught up with him would be hard to believe. But something had occurred, else Gorman would have shown up at the Hanlon place by that time.

He'd go first to where he and Gorman had split up, and then ride in the direction Ed had taken. Of course Gorman could have changed, swung off onto an entirely different course fifty yards later, but that was a chance he'd have to take. At least he'd be in the right area.

Sullen, grim faced, Turk Roper rode on. He was getting close to Muleshoe, he realized, for he could smell the charred wood, and smoke was still lingering among the trees. He should be careful, he thought, cautioning himself, for there likely would still be Muleshoe riders searching about, but he didn't give the self-imposed warning much thought. The important thing was to find Gorman.

He reached the point where he had last seen Ed—a large pile of rocks upon which rabbit brush had made a ragged, gray-green crown. The old man had gone right, and Turk had swung left. Not halting, Roper at once turned into the route his friend had taken, riding slowly now as he cast his eyes from side to side looking for sign that would tell him he was on the right trail.

He had strung along with Ed and Virg Bratton willingly enough when they agreed to throw in with Cameron. It had looked like a chance for some excitement while picking up a few dollars in wages. He still wasn't exactly sure he knew what was in Cameron's mind, but it had to do with running Sid Mason out of the country—not killing him—and forcing him to give back the land he'd euchred some folks out of.

Just what was in it for Cameron he didn't know. He'd had a ranch, sure, and some cattle, and this Sid Mason had ended up with both—or maybe it was just the cattle. And then there was the blond woman who'd come to warn them about the raid. She was Mason's wife, but it was plenty plain that once she had meant a lot to John Cameron. If he—

Two quick gunshots brought Turk Roper to sudden attention. They were not close, came from perhaps a mile or so to the east. But it could be no one else but Ed Gorman. With Virg Bratton dead the old man was the only other one of Cameron's party still in the woods.

At once, Roper dug spurs into his horse and started for what he figured was the source of the reports. He rode as fast as was possible through the brush and trees, and when he reached a place he estimated was somewhere near where the shots came from, pulled his horse down to a walk and proceeded more quietly.

A dozen yards and again Roper halted. Three horses were drawn up in the trees at the edge of what looked to be a small clearing. One of them was Ed Gorman's. Quickly cutting back around in order to keep in the brush, Roper, taut, his dark features a hard-cornered mask, eyes little more than slits, circled in behind the animals and dismounted.

He could hear voices, as gun in hand, he began to work his way toward the clearing. Reaching its edge, he dropped low, peered through the screen of brush. Anger shook him, and a curse ripped from his throat.

Three Muleshoe riders—one of them Bear Kugan—had Gorman, hands tied behind his back, in the saddle on a horse. A rope was around his neck, and as Turk watched, one of the trio threw its loose end over the limb of a cottonwood tree. Ed Gorman had been wounded—twice it appeared. The blood on his leg was dark and crusted, that on his chest looked to be fresh.

"Get him up," Bear Kugan said as the rider with the rope fastened it to a second, nearby tree. "Give that horse a kick so's we can start this bird to swinging."

"Turn him loose—you sonsofbitches!" Roper snarled, stepping abruptly into the clearing.

Kugan and the other men wheeled. Gorman slumped in the saddle, head down. He looked around weakly. A grin split his lips.

"It's one of them others working for Cameron!" Kugan said. "Hell, he ain't going to shoot. He does, it'll spook that horse, and that pal of his'll be walking on air."

"Maybe," Roper said coldly, "but you sure won't be around to see it 'cause you'll be dead." Moving slowly, carefully, he eased in to where the hanging rope was anchored. Reaching down, he jerked the tag end of the slip knot. The rope slackened and fell free. Gorman sagged lower in the saddle.

"Get him off that horse!" Roper ordered in a scarcely controlled voice.

There was a long breathless moment, and then Kugan, eyes snapping with anger, touched his two companions with a glance and started to comply with Turk's flat, no-quarter command. Midway, Bear suddenly threw himself to one side and dragged out his pistol.

"Shoot!" he shouted at the riders. "Shoot the bas—"

Bear Kugan never finished what he intended to say.

Roper, cool as winter's wind, put a bullet in his head, spun, and downed a second man before the Muleshoe rider could trigger his weapon. The third man flung up his hands, pivoted, and started for his horse at a run. Roper, smoke drifting lazily about him, leveled his gun at the retreating rider's back, then, soaring anger spent, lowered the weapon. Motionless, he waited until the quick pounding of a horse leaving the area fast indicated the Muleshoe man was gone and was no longer a source of danger.

Moving quickly, Roper hurried to where Ed Gorman was slumped in the saddle. Reaching up, he lifted his friend off the horse and set him gently on the ground. Taking out his knife, he cut the rawhide strip that bound Ed's wrists together.

"Old man, you sure have got yourself in a mess this time," he said softly. "Figured something was wrong. Reason I come looking for you."

Gorman managed a grin. "Sort of thought you'd be showing up," he said haltingly. "Got myself winged right after we split up. Hid out here in the brush, but them polecats found me. Tried getting away but they—they put another slug in my hide. Then danged if that Kugan didn't get the idea to hang me—string me up."

"I reckon I got here just in time," Turk said. "I'll go fetch your horse and get you back to the cabin. That gal friend of Cameron's is a fair to middling doc."

"There ain't no hurry," Gorman said, his voice dropping lower. Words were now coming with more difficulty. "I ain't for certain I can set a saddle—way things are working out."

"Hell, you'll be good as new once that gal gets her hands on you!" Roper declared. Rising, he stepped over

Bear Kugan's body and dropped back to where the horses were waiting. Releasing them all, Turk grasped the reins of Gorman's, collected those of his own, and led them into the clearing where his friend had laid back on the grassy ground.

"You for sure you can't set a saddle?" Roper asked, halting nearby. "If you can't, I expect I can rig up a drag, using brush and some of them dead fellow's clothes."

"Never mind," Gorman murmured weakly. His eyes were closed, and there was a slackness to his windburned features. "I don't reckon—I ought—ought to plan—on going nowheres. Just you set yourself down—here—close by."

Roper swore deeply, furiously under his breath. That Ed Gorman was actually dying was difficult to believe. Sure—everybody cashed in eventually—but Ed, here and now?

"All right, old man," he said. "I'll be—"

"Stand easy, Turk—"

At the quiet, almost friendly admonition coming from the fringe of the clearing, Roper froze.

"I'm taking you in for murder—got you dead to rights. Them two bodies is all the proof I need."

Deke Henry . . . Also known as Nate Stanwyck . . . A fresh rush of anger heightened Roper's sense of frustration. The sonofabitch had sure picked the wrong time to show up—and he'd play hell taking anybody in to his damned jail.

"Get your hands up, Turk—and turn around real slow."

"Just as you say, Deke," Roper murmured in a voice barely audible, and began to pivot.

In the next fragment of time Roper buckled, lunged to one side. The pistol that had been nestling in the oiled holster at his side was magically in his hand. It roared in the same breath as did that of the man who called himself Nate Stanwyck.

Turk flinched as a bullet seared across his neck, but he remained crouched, smoking weapon poised while Stanwyck twisted slowly about and fell heavily from the back of his horse. Only then did Turk Roper draw himself erect.

Eyes on the lifeless figure of the lawman, he punched out the spent cartridges in the cylinder of his gun, reloaded it from the few remaining in his belt, and shoved it into its holster. Coming about at once, he crossed to where Ed Gorman lay.

"Now I reckon we can get back to the shack without no more bother," he said, "but we best do it in a hurry. Like as not we'll have a whole passel of them Muleshoe gunnies down on us soon as that fellow gets to the ranch and does some talking. You ready?"

Ed Gorman made no reply. He was beyond hurry, or caring.

CHAPTER 15

Cameron roused slowly. He was sitting in a back corner of the shack, having eaten a bit of the food Ketty Griffin had brought and treated himself to a drink from the little that still remained in one of Turk Roper's bottles of whiskey.

Movement sent a stab of pain shooting through his left arm. Cursing softy, he pulled himself to his feet. The aches and soreness from the beating he'd taken from Bear Kugan and other Muleshoe riders were still pronounced, but he paid little attention to those discomforts; he was more concerned with the stiffness of his wounded arm.

Drawing away from the wall, he began to move his arm, gradually breaking the restrictive stiffness, flexing the member slowly, his jaw set against the pain. It was a good thing it was his left arm, he thought; the trouble with Sid Mason and his men was far from over! He could expect to use his gun again—probably before the day was over. With the help of Ed Gorman, Turk, and Virg Bratton—God rest him—he'd crippled Muleshoe badly, but Sid Mason was far from finished.

Gorman . . . Was he dead, too? Cameron paused, stood quietly working the fingers of his left hand. How many men were dead? A tremor passed through him. Five—six—perhaps more. It was difficult to tell about the encounter at Mason's; they had set fire to everything that would burn, had quickly been enveloped in dust and smoke, and with darkness also a factor, there had been no way of knowing just how many men had gone down.

But he had Sid Mason looking at his hole card, there was no doubt about that. Sid would have to take stock of himself and decide what next he should do. Would he be willing to admit he'd been beaten, dispose of his holdings by quit claim deeds and sales, and move on? That was the price.

"I reckon he knows now that I meant what I said," Cameron muttered aloud.

But he doubted Mason would be ready to quit. True, his losses were heavy, but Sid was no greenhorn; he'd ridden the river trail before and could take care of himself; he had men like Bear Kugan and Ben Lancaster on his payroll just to relieve him of such disagreeable chores as evictions, browbeatings, and the like. He could handle it all himself, and would.

His arm had loosened up slightly. Cameron began to increase the exercising, working now more from the elbow. A spot of red appeared on the bandage Ketty had applied, as the wound opened and blood soaked through. He ignored that, also. Hell, he'd been hurt worse brawling inside the pen! Once he'd had a knife—one made from a piece of barrel hoop—stuck half through him, and lived. What could a lousy bullet wound—

Cameron's thoughts came to a stop. There was the sound of horses outside—more than one, therefore it wouldn't

be Ketty returning with the ammunition they would be
needing; it could be Turk and Gorman, of course—or it
might be some of the Muleshoe bunch, remembering the
old cabin and coming to have a look.

Drawing his pistol, Cameron stepped quietly to the
door, and with the fingers of his injured arm, opened the
flimsy panel a crack. A curse slipped from his lips, and a
heaviness settled over him. It was Roper, and he had
Gorman's lifeless body hung across the saddle of the
horse trailing behind.

Holstering his weapon, Cameron stepped hurriedly
outside. Roper, dismounting, turned to face him.

"They was going to string him up!" Turk said in a low,
bitter voice that trembled with anger. "Was already bad
shot, but them bastards—that Bear Kugan and a couple
of others—was going to string him up. Had the rope
around his neck and flung over a limb when I got there.
Stopped them. Two of them for good—one of them was
Kugan."

"Kugan's dead?"

"Yeh . . . Brought the old man back with me so's I
could bury him right. Sure wasn't leaving him there with
them two, and that tinhorn marshal for the buzzards to—"

"Marshal?" Cameron echoed. "Nate Stanwyck was
there?"

"Name ain't Stanwyck, it's Deke Henry. Come for me
after he run into that jasper I let go—one of them Muleshoe
cowhands that was stringing up Ed. Said he was taking
me in for murder. Was a little slow trying."

Cameron shook his head slowly. He was thinking of
what Aaron Wilson had said—that Cameron was a
firebrand, and that he'd likely set the whole valley afire.
He had countered with the remark that perhaps that was

THE RENEGADE GUN 159

what the country needed. It had sounded right to him then, but he hadn't figured on so much blood being spilled.

And now he could chalk up the name of Nate Stanwyck, or Deke Henry, whichever was his right name—a lawman—to the list. But maybe he shouldn't feel responsible for the marshal's death. There had been something bad and personal between him and Turk Roper—something out of the past.

Noticing Roper starting to lift Gorman's body off the horse, Cameron stepped forward to assist. The gunman waved him off.

"Sort of like to do this myself. Besides you ain't in no shape to do nothing much—and don't go sorrowing over Deke Henry. He was a no-good, lying four-flusher," Roper said, hanging Gorman's stiffening body over a shoulder. A somewhat smaller man, he staggered a bit under the load, and as Cameron again offered to help, Turk for the second time shook him off.

"Seen a pretty deep gully right over there at the edge of the yard," he said, starting to move off. "Aim to wrap him in his blanket and plant him and his belongings there. Can cave in dirt and rocks on top of him so's the varmints won't bother him none."

Cameron turned at once, entered the shack, and obtained the wool cover. When he retraced his steps to the yard, Roper had crossed to the wash he'd mentioned, and was getting Gorman's saddlebags to lay with the body. Spreading out the blanket, he placed his friend on it, wrapped the covering tightly about the lean shape, and then lowered it into the gully. As Cameron stood by watching, Turk caved in the dirt sides of the wash, and afterward finished making a grave by carrying in larger rocks and piling them onto the loose soil.

"Reckon he'll sleep good now," Roper said, dusting off his hands. He stood for a full minute looking down at the mound, a faraway, lost expression on his dark face. Then, "So long, old man," he added, and turned away.

Moving back to where the two horses stood, Turk gathered up the reins and led them into the brush where Cameron had picketed his mount. That done, he rejoined Cameron, and together they entered the shack.

"How's that arm of yours doing?" Roper asked, taking up his bottle of whiskey and having a drink.

"Stiff," Cameron replied. "Been working with it, trying to loosen it up. Doing some good."

Turk emptied the bottle of whiskey, dug about in his blanket for the other. "Reckon you're wondering about me and Deke. Little something that happened a long time ago. I was a lawman at the time."

Cameron nodded. "I see."

"Yeh, was young then, all full of fire, and aiming to be the best damned lawman that ever rode the river. Deke, he was a—"

The quick beat of a horse coming into the yard put an end to whatever it was Turk Roper intended to say. With Cameron a step ahead of him, Roper hurried to the door—left open now to relieve the rising heat—and glanced out.

"It's the gal," Roper said, slipping his pistol back into the holster and turning back.

Cameron waited for Ketty to tie her horse alongside the others, and met her at the edge of the house. She smiled at first look at him, and then as she handed over the two boxes of cartridges, frowned at the sight of the bloody bandage on his arm.

"You've been out," she began accusingly.

"Nope, was trying to loosen up my arm . . . Ed Gorman's dead."

Ketty looked down, and as they started to enter the shack, said to both men, "I'm sorry. I liked Ed."

"Reckon most folks did," Turk replied.

"I've got something to tell you," Ketty continued, putting Cameron on the upturned keg and beginning to unwrap the stained cloth circling his arm. "Not sure if it's good or bad."

"Not much left to happen that would be bad," Cameron said indifferently.

"Lige Davidson stopped me when I was in town. Said to tell you that he'd been talking around, and he and some of the other ranchers are ready to throw in with you."

"Beginning to see the light now that we've all but put this Mason out of business," Roper said with a sarcastic laugh. "We could've used their help last night."

Cameron made no comment. It was more or less as he had expected; the first move against Sid Mason—even though it was for their benefit—had to be made by him. If it worked out successfully, all well and good—he'd find he had plenty of support. If not, well, it had been something of his own choosing. Human nature being what it was would cause them to look at it in that light.

"Lige said that he and Claude Ivey and Tom Lear wanted to meet with you at your place. They hope to bring along some other men, but they wanted to get word to you so's you'd be expecting them."

"My place," Cameron said in a doubtful voice. "Be better here—"

"What I told Lige, but he said the word had already been sent out, and he couldn't change it. Do you want me to go back, tell him that you—"

"No, we've got them thinking straight about Sid Mason, so we better not do something that might cause them to change their minds and back off. When are we supposed to meet?"

"Noon, or thereabouts," Ketty replied, finished with replacing the stained bandage.

Cameron nodded, handed one of the boxes of cartridges to Roper, and began to fill the empty loops of his own belt from the other.

"Doesn't give us a lot of time," he said, "but we'll make it. Now, Ketty, I want you to head back to town and wait for me."

Ketty smiled. "I'd as soon go along with you—"

"Too risky. It's a cinch Mason's still got his bunch combing the brush for us—surprised one of them hasn't thought of this place—and I won't take a chance on your getting hurt."

"All right, I'll be there waiting for you—like you want," Ketty said, and stepping in close, kissed him lightly on the cheek, smiled, and hurried out the doorway.

"Like I was saying, I was the marshal in this town over Kansas way when I had a run-in with Deke Henry."

Roper had taken up the account of his trouble with Nate Stanwyck a short time later while they were riding to the rendezvous with Lige Davidson and the other ranchers and homesteaders now willing to take a stand against

Mason. They kept well within the brush in the event there were Muleshoe men in the area.

"Was all full of righteousness and goodness, and figured I was about the best that ever hung on a star. One day I got called to a saloon—little two-bit outfit—where there was a ruckus going on. Got there and found Deke Henry—I didn't know him by name then—there with three or four friends. They was busting up things real bad. I hollered for them to back off, or I'd jug the lot of them.

"Wasn't watching my backside, and one of them got in behind me and buffaloed me good. When I come to Deke had me with a rope around my middle and my hands tied back of me. He told his friends to shuck my boots and pants, and when they done it, he pushed me out into the open.

"Got on his horse then, and started down the street with me stumbling along after him at the end of that rope, with nothing on but my drawers and shirt. He went back and forth about half a dozen times with everybody in town standing around laughing at me. He finally got tired of having his fun and turned me loose, and him and his friends rode on.

"Well, that finished me being a lawman. Every time somebody around there looked at me they'd start laughing, remembering what I looked like trotting up and down the street in my drawers and bare feet—and I guess I sure was a mighty funny sight. Just couldn't face folks so I handed in my star and moved on. But before Deke rode off that day I told him if I ever seen him again, I'd kill him. And I did."

Roper hesitated, wiped at the sweat on his forehead

with the back of his wrist. "Kind of funny now, me being a lawman then, him being one now."

Cameron shifted on his saddle. Although the buckskin was moving at a walk, the motion was sending pain through Cameron's arm with every step, and he was having a difficult time finding comfort.

"You ever pin on a badge again?"

Turk said, "Nope, never. Had all I wanted of being the law. Was just about to ride back into town that first day we come to your place and found you all beat up by them Muleshoe gunnies, and see for sure if it'd been Deke I seen standing in front of the marshal's office, wearing a star. But Gorman kept telling me not to get all fired up and maybe let myself in for a hanging. He said I ought to just sort of wait, and maybe things would take care of themselves. I reckon they did. We threw in with you—and I got my chance to square up with Deke."

Cameron again stirred about on the saddle as he sought to ease his pain. They were not far from the J-Bar-C now.

"I'm obliged to you and the others for siding in with me. Couldn't have done much without your help," he said, and after a moment added, "Feel mighty bad about Gorman and Virg, though."

Turk Roper shrugged. "I reckon that's all right. We all figured to cash in that way, living the kind of life we was. Don't need to fault yourself none. If it hadn't happened here, it would've somewheres else someday. And I expect Gorman and the kid would figure it was worth it, after us seeing what this Mason's like."

Cameron brushed at his jaw, frowning. "Been wondering about that—wondering if maybe what I'm trying to do is costing too much. When I think of the men that've been killed—on both sides—I—"

"No call for you to look at it that way. I'm being honest when I say I sort of misdoubted you and what you claimed you'd set your mind to doing, at first, but I see now that you meant it just like you said because there ain't nothing in it for you except the satisfaction of seeing Mason busted and drove out. And if there ain't men like you to come along now and then who'll put a stop to the Sid Masons, why this country ain't never going to amount to anything."

Cameron started to reply, instead raised a hand for silence. He thought he'd heard a shout from somewhere on ahead. Turk looked at him questioningly.

"Something bothering you?"

In that next moment a pistol shot flatted hollowly across the hot, still day.

Immediately Cameron put spurs to the buckskin. "Shot come from my place—I think!" he said as the horse broke into a fast run.

With Turk Roper at his side he reached the edge of the clearing in which the ruins of his ranch lay. As they broke into the open, heedless of any Muleshoe riders, a deep fear had sprung to life in John Cameron's mind. At once he saw that it was well founded.

In front of what had been the bunkhouse sprawled Lige Davidson. Astride his horse nearby, pistol still in his hand, was Sid Mason. Beyond him a bit was the gunman, Ben Lancaster.

Turk swore. "That dead man the rancher who was coming to see you?"

"That's him—Lige Davidson," Cameron replied tautly. Pistol out, he sent the buckskin rushing straight for Mason and Lancaster, still unaware of his presence.

But only for that moment. They heard, and then saw

Cameron and Roper bearing down on them from the brush. At once they wheeled and started to rush off in the opposite direction. Turk's pistol blasted—the report so close to Cameron that it briefly deafened him. Lancaster buckled forward over his saddle, bounced drunkenly along for a few strides, and then fell to the ground.

Cameron, a towering anger boiling through him, snapped a shot at Mason, as Roper seemingly by mutual understanding withheld shooting at Muleshoe's owner. The bullet grazed the rancher, causing him to jerk to one side. The sudden change confused the big bay horse he was riding. He cut short as the reins dragged at the bit between his teeth. Abruptly confronted by dense brush, the horse veered again, stumbled, and went to his knees, throwing Mason from the saddle.

Cameron, rushing across the yard, spurred the buckskin recklessly into the brush. He could not see Sid Mason, but knew the man was somewhere close by—and beyond the bay, now back on his feet and trembling from the fall.

Pulling the fractious buckskin to a halt, Cameron listened. He could hear nothing, and then it occurred to him that sitting in the saddle, silhouetted above the brush, he was offering himself to Mason as an easy target. At once he left the back of the gelding, swearing deeply as pain rocketed through him when his heels hit solid ground.

The rattle and crash of dry brush on ahead came to him as he recovered his balance. He realized it was Sid Mason running. Gun in hand, Cameron threw himself in pursuit. He could see nothing of the rancher, but left arm hanging at his side, muscles drawn tight to minimize the pain, he hurried on. Branches slapped at him, caught at his clothing, left their stinging mark on his bruised face. Once he stumbled, went to his knees. Cursing, pain hammering at him, sweat bathing his body, he lunged back upright and rushed on.

Sid Mason was not going to escape. He was going to pay for all the misery he had brought about, all the deaths he had caused. That determination was like a burning brand within John Cameron; he would stop Mason— kill him—put him where he could never again harm anyone.

Motion off to his left caught Cameron's quick attention. It was Turk Roper, keeping pace with him. Cameron ran on. He was now sucking hard for wind, knew Mason would be no better off, and tiring also. And then Muleshoe's owner came into view as he spurted into a small clearing. Immediately Cameron brought up his pistol, thumb drawing back the hammer as he did.

But he didn't want Sid Mason dead. That would be too good for the rancher. He had to stay alive, be forced to undo all the wrong he'd committed, return the land he'd usurped by one means or another, so the valley could revert to the peaceful, friendly land it once was.

Lowering his weapon, John Cameron plunged on through the brush.

CHAPTER 16

~~~~~~

Darcy Mason, leaning forward on the seat of her somewhat fire-damaged buggy, urged the horse on with the tip
of her whip. She had to reach John Cameron's place,
warn him that he would be riding into an ambush.

Manuelita, the Mexican cook she had brought with her
when she'd sold the restaurant and married Sid, had
overheard one of the riders talking to her husband. He'd
been in town that morning, had been nearby when Lige
Davidson told Ketty Griffin to have John meet him at the
J-Bar-C around noon. Others were to come, Davidson had
said. They planned to line up with Cameron against
Sid.

It was the situation Sid had been hoping for—a chance
to trap Cameron, silence him—and any other malcontent
present—once and for all time. Sid had gone to find Ben
Lancaster, his right-hand man since Bear Kugan had
gotten killed. As soon as Sid had departed their tempo-
rary quarters in the house of the ranch foreman, which
had escaped the fire, she had sent Manuelita into the

yard with instructions for the hostler to hitch up her horse and buggy and have them ready.

When it was, Darcy had driven off at top speed for the J-Bar-C. She didn't know where John Cameron would be found at the moment; he and his men were probably somewhere in the hills awaiting an opportunity to strike again—this time at Sid's herds of cattle, Sid had assumed; but there was no doubt that John would keep his appointment with Davidson and whoever else planned to come, and that was where she could meet and warn him.

She was getting near to the J-Bar-C—or what remained of it. Darcy could always tell she was close by the big cottonwood trees that grew a short distance from the house. They served as a sort of landmark for her.

Abruptly a man burst from the brush growing along the edge of the road and charged out in front of her, arms waving frantically. Fear and then surprise coursed through Darcy. It was Sid. Clothing torn, dusty, gasping for breath, he motioned for her to stop.

"Get over!" he shouted when she did. Jerking the lines from her hands, he crowded onto the seat beside her. "I've got to—"

"Mason!"

John Cameron's voice cut into Sid's words. Darcy glanced off to the side, saw Cameron, pistol up and leveled at her husband.

Sid froze. She could sense the fear that gripped him, saw it in the tenseness of his body as he stiffened, and slowly began to bend forward.

"Throw down your gun!"

At Cameron's harsh command, Sid's hand slid to the holster on his hip, came up with the handle of the weapon between the tips of his fingers. Holding it aside, he allowed it to fall to the ground.

At that John Cameron lowered the pistol he'd been pointing to his side, and started toward the buggy.

"You shot Lige Davidson," he called out as he approached. "I aim to see you hang for that—but first we're going into town and have Aaron Wilson make up some quit claim deeds on the land you—"

"The hell I am!" Sid yelled, and snatched up the rifle lying at his feet on the floorboards of the buggy. Jacking a cartridge into its chamber, he whirled and leveled it at Cameron, who was only then reaching for his weapon.

Darcy cried a warning but before it left her lips a pistol cracked sharply from the brush beyond Cameron. Mason jolted as a bullet drove into him. His fingers relaxed, and the rifle dropped, striking the side of the buggy and then falling to the ground. Sid was perfectly still, seemingly staring off down the road, and then he slumped back into the seat.

Cameron hurried up, and coming from the brush a few yards farther on was Turk—pistol still in his hand as if he expected to have to use it again. Darcy looked at the man who was her husband. She felt no grief, no sorrow, only a sort of numbness. Many times she had wondered how she could have married him; that question presented itself to her again.

"Darcy—I'm sorry," she heard John Cameron say. "Not how I wanted it to end."

She shook her head. "Knowing Sid, this is the only way it could end," she said. "He was too proud, I guess the word is arrogant, to face up to what was ahead for him."

"Expect you're right . . . If you like, Turk and me will look after him, take him into town."

Darcy smiled tightly, gathered up the lines. "No, it's my place to do it . . . Will you be coming?"

"Soon as I get my horse."

Near sundown, Cameron, in company with Turk Roper, entered Wolf Springs. He was leading the horse Lige Davidson had been riding. The rancher's body lay across the saddle. Roper had the horse of Ben Lancaster trailing him, with the gunman's slack shape hung over it. They rode directly to Sweeney's stable where Cameron asked the livery barn owner to take charge and make the necessary arrangements.

Coming about then, Cameron started for the High Ridge Saloon & Restaurant. Ketty was standing in front with several men who had witnessed his and Roper's arrival. Darcy Mason's buggy was drawn up before the bank, and as he glanced toward it, the woman and Aaron Wilson came out into the street. The banker raised an arm, beckoned to Cameron. Others were putting in an appearance now—Kurtzman from the bakery, John's onetime friend George Morgan, Pete Major, Zeke Taylor. All moved toward the bank.

"I reckon you've got some business to tend to," Roper said, maintaining his course for the saloon. "If you're wanting me for something, I'll be in the High Ridge wetting my whistle."

Cameron said, "We'll get together later," and turned to the bank and the group now awaiting him there. He looked again to Ketty. She had not stirred, but was hesitating as if not certain she would be welcome at whatever the meeting was about. Cameron motioned to the woman, and waited until she was beside him. Together, they continued across the dusty street.

"Mrs. Mason's got something she wants to say," Wilson greeted Cameron. "Figured you being at the bottom of all this—this—" The banker hesitated, groped for words.

"Trouble—and killing," Cameron supplied quietly.

"Exactly!" Wilson snapped. "Right now there's a big question in my mind. Do you figure it was worth it—all the deaths—all the blood spilled?"

"Not what we're here to talk about, Aaron," Morgan declared, waving the banker aside. "And I reckon only time will answer that question. Point is, Cameron had the guts to step in and change the way things were going. Now we can get back to how it once was, thanks to him—and to what Darcy—Mrs. Mason—aims to do."

Cameron could feel Darcy's eyes upon him, and returned her gaze. She smiled, and then glanced about.

"I'm Muleshoe now," she began in a firm voice. "Anybody who feels he was cheated in the past by my husband, or who wants back his land, has only to come tell me so. I'll make things right.

"There'll be changes at Muleshoe. I intend to rebuild it, hire on new hands. I'm hoping John Cameron will take on the job as my new foreman."

Cameron felt Ketty's hand tighten on his arm, and sensed the withdrawal that seemed to possess her. The thought: *you've won, you've beaten Mason, done what you set out to do, now take the rewards*, passed through his mind.

"We've—the town's got an offer to make, too," George Morgan said. "John, we know we've treated you mighty shabby, and now we'd like a chance to make up for it.

We got together and decided to offer you the job as our marshal, along with help in rebuilding your ranch."

Ketty was still tense beside him, awaiting his answer, his decision. The offers were both fine opportunities, either one a chance to get back on his feet, become somebody in the valley. But he knew intuitively how Ketty felt, and thus it was a matter of priorities, of which counted most.

"What do you say?" Kurtzman asked in his thickly accented voice. "You will take the job as marshal, yes?"

Cameron glanced at Ketty. Her face was tipped down, her eyes partly closed. She would not question what he did, but he knew where her preference lay.

"Obliged to you, George—and the rest of you for the offer," he said, bringing his attention back to the storekeeper, "but the job's not for me. There's a man over in the saloon by the name of Turk Roper. Talk to him. Just could be you can get him to take it."

Cameron turned to Darcy. A smile parted her lips, and her eyes were bright with expectancy.

"Have to turn you down, too," he said, and felt the relief that coursed through the girl beside him. "Ketty and me are pulling out soon as I can sell my herd—heading on west. Aim to find a place that suits us, and start living again."

Exciting SIGNET Westerns by Ernest Haycox

(0451)

☐ **STARLIGHT RIDER** (123468—$2.25)*
☐ **BUGLES IN THE AFTERNOON** (114671—$2.25)*
☐ **CHAFEE OF ROARING HORSE** (114248—$1.95)*
☐ **RETURN OF A FIGHTER** (094190—$1.75)
☐ **RIDERS WEST** (099796—$1.95)*
☐ **SUNDOWN JIM** (096762—$1.75)*
☐ **TRAIL SMOKE** (112822—$1.95)*
☐ **TRAIL TOWN** (097793—$1.95)*
☐ **CANYON PASSAGE** (117824—$2.25)*
☐ **DEEP WEST** (118839—$2.25)*
☐ **FREE GRASS** (118383—$2.25)*
☐ **HEAD OF THE MOUNTAIN** (120817—$2.50)*
☐ **SIGNET DOUBLE WESTERN: ACTION BY NIGHT and TROUBLE SHOOTER** (123891—$3.50)*
☐ **SIGNET DOUBLE WESTERN: SADDLE & RIDE and THE FEUDISTS** (094670—$1.95)
☐ **SIGNET DOUBLE WESTERN: ALDER GULCH and A RIDER OF THE HIGH MESA** (122844—$3.50)*

Prices slightly higher in Canada

SIGNET Westerns by Lewis B. Patten

Buy them at your local

bookstore or use coupon

on next page for ordering.

SIGNET Westerns You'll Enjoy